Cash Keepers 2

Like A Boss

A "Dope-Tale" By:
D'Shon Major

Platform Bookhouse Publishing
P.O Box 252
Del Valle, Tx 78617

Printed in the United States of America

Published by:
Platform Bookhouse Publishing

ISBN: 979-8-9944488-4-7

Library of Congress Control Number: 2026912761

Email: platformbookhousepublishing@gmail.com

Website: pbhpublishing.com

Check us out on our social media platforms:
TikTok: @pbptok02
Facebook: Platform Bookhouse Publishing
Instagram: Platform Bookhouse Publishing

Author's Note

What Is a Cash Keeper?

A lot of people think they understand what a Cash Keeper is... or isn't. They hear Cash Keeper and immediately think of money-the hustle, the shine, the glory-but not the story. But if that's all you see, then you're missing the bigger picture. A Cash Keeper ain't just somebody getting money or stacking it. It's somebody who levels up and understands everything that comes with it. Because money brings power-but it also brings problems. Problems that show up at your doorstep with choices that don't always come with clean morals attached. And once you step into that world, everything around you starts revealing itself for what it really is... not what you thought it was. A Cash Keeper stands in the middle of that chaos-and holds it together. So as you flip these pages, pay attention to the decisions. The risks. The moments where everything could've gone sideways-and sometimes did. That's what this life is about. Not just chasing a bag... but living with whatever it costs to keep it. Because at the end of the day-Cash keeping ain't just a hustle. It's a way of life.

-D'Shon Major
Platform Bookhouse Publishing
Home of the Streets

Dedication

This book is dedicated to the hustlers (Cash Keepers) who learned survival before they learned peace. To those who keep going when quitting is easier. This is for you.

INTRODUCTION

In celebration of a year's worth of successful hustling, Wild Bill and his running mate Slim were posted in the VIP section of Club Vanity, baller status on full display. Expensive champagne bottles dropped like water. The two were lightweight tipsy, but smothered themselves in confidence and felt untouchable now that the days of poor-man hustling were behind them.

"Damn. It's women everywhere in here," Wild Bill said, throwing his hands toward the ceiling. "You gotta be gayer than RuPaul to leave without something."

Slim laughed. "I don't know about you, but I'll be between foreign thighs before sunrise." He pulled out his phone and texted Kennisha - a woman he'd caught feelings for, even though he still tried to keep his player image intact.

"Yo, you talkin' 'bout that fine thang you rolled up with last weekend?" Wild Bill leaned closer, peeking over Slim's shoulder. "Put me on her friend. All the bad ones got fine homegirls."

"Dang, peepin' Tom," Slim joked. "Relax. Let me see what she say first."

A minute later, Kennisha responded. She and her homegirl were chilling and could use some company. She sent the address.

Slim grinned. "Let's blow this spot. We got a hit."

In unison, they finished off the last of the liquor, let the empty bottles thud against the floor, and made their way down the stairs and out the side exit where their cars sat parked side-by-side.

Slim pulled off first in a brand-new Dodge Charger sitting high on 24-inch rims. Wild Bill followed close behind in a candy-coated Chrysler 300, both cars weaved through traffic like they owned the city. The liquor played its part, but most of the recklessness came from being young, paid, and fearless.

They pulled into the Motel 6 lot and parked poolside. Laughing too loud for one in the morning, they made their way up the short flight of stairs toward room 227, passing a blunt back and forth. Slim adjusted the pistol sagging beneath his True Religion jeans and knocked.

The door cracked open.

Queen stood there.

She eyed them slowly before stepping aside. "That was fast."

Once inside, the door shut hard behind them. "Sorry," she added softly.

"It's cool, Wild Bill said, removing his hand from where his burner rested. He didn't recognize the setup - not yet. But the play had been in motion for months.

Ever since Slim and Queen crossed paths at Wild Bill's birthday party the year before, the pieces had been moving. Queen had played her role perfectly. She painted Slim a picture of distraction while another plan brewed beneath the surface.

The original trap had Wild Bill's name stamped on it, but his trigger-happy sidekick latched on to the bait. Queen even sampled his package and gave him head. All because he'd soon met his doom…tonight.

Since Wild Bill and Slim clipped the Traffic House for money and drugs, they had been moving weight on the southside with the assumption that everything was good.
Young Ham knew better.

He had convinced his partners to stay patient, and let the heat cool instead of striking while the stove was still hot. If they moved too soon, they might as well have walked into the police station and turned themselves in.

"Listen close," Young Ham warned. "Wild Bill and his people ain't to be taken lightly. They peel caps for real. So if it goes left... shoot first."

"Man, I ain't barring no nigga that stand and piss like I do," Youngin' said, wiping down his weapon.

Smiley turned and eyeballed Youngin'. "This ain't about you, homey. Don't let that heroic shit get you...or us killed."

"Yo, chill." Young Ham said. "These clowns done slipped. Ain't no crossing CKC and think we turning the other cheek like Jesus."

Now the time had come.

Twenty-five minutes later, the Cash Keepers stepped out of room 228 onto the balcony. Young Ham counted to three with his fingers and slid a key card into room 227's slot.

The red light turned green.

$ $ $ $ $

The door bust open. The only light inside came from the television. Slim stood at the edge of the bed with his pants around his ankles, digging in Queen from the back with rhythm and intensity. He was lost in his own pleasure, unaware that his final moment had already been written.

Gunfire exploded through the room.

Slim didn't have time to react. Hollow-points from Young Ham's Beretta tore through him before he could reach for his weapon. Queen dropped to the floor, clearing herself from the line of fire.

Across the room, Wild Bill reacted on instinct. He rolled off the bed just as a .45 slug ripped past where his head had been. He hit the floor firing, squeezing off wild shots from the .44 in his grip.

Young Ham and Smiley dove behind an oak-stained dresser as rounds penetrated drywall and splintered wood.

Wild Bill kept shooting.

Then everything shifted.

While Wild Bill's focus stayed locked on the Cash Keepers, Kenya rose quietly from the side of the bed where she had fallen when the shooting started.

He never saw her coming. She flashed the razor once and cut him ear-to-ear in a single swipe.

Wild Bill's weapon slipped from his grip as he clutched his throat, collapsing backward into the wall. Blood streaked down the cream-colored paint as he slid to his knees.

Smiley stepped out and put two final rounds in his chest. Silence swallowed the room.

The Change Up

Two weeks had passed since the double homicide at the hotel. The names of the dead bodies were still circulating in whispers, but there were no solid leads or suspects in connection with the unsolved murders.

The heat on the streets from one-time had calmed. Every participant of the game that dabbled in violence had decided that Wild Bill's murder was getting what he deserved.

Young Ham rested both hands behind his head as the midday sun broke across the California king-size bed. He stared up at the wide screen plasma hanging from the ceiling, but his mind roamed elsewhere.

The call moments ago had ruined a needed relaxing, settling in like unwanted drama on a good-day. Someone other than Franco was using his connect's phone, talking loose and reckless - as though they were untouchable. The caller demanded his presence in Houston before nightfall. Young Ham tried sliding in a few words, but the line went dead.

Where the hell is Franco, Young Ham thought, and why is somebody using his phone? When in the beginning he straight up told me not to bring no one else into the business.

"Babe, what's on your mind?" Monique said, sauntering in and breaking up his thoughts. "You look like you're in a heated chess game."

Although they were officially under lock and key as a couple, Monique remained in the blind about his day-to-day operations. Kindly enough, she assumed his wealth came from his mom's passing, combined with the money from selling Maw-maw's house when she died last year. Being that she never questioned how he balled so hard, he let it ride too, and kept the streets and its ugly ways far from reach.

"I'm good, Moni," he said, acting unbothered. "But say, I'm 'bout to take care of some business later, and I'll be back before tonight."

"Alright, but I'm running by the office to download a few cases I need. Then I'm coming back to start dinner."

"Cool." Young Ham got up to shower. "If I'm not back in time, put me a plate in the microwave."

By the time he finished washing up and getting dressed, Monique was already gone. He decided on driving something modest and not too flashy - in other words, blend in with traffic. He grabbed the keys to the CT-6 and hit the highway.

$ $ $ $ $

An expensive list of exotic cars lined bumper-to-bumper along the off-white mansion's circular driveway. After driving in and finding nowhere to park, Young Ham brushed aside the inconvenience and left his vehicle in the middle of the lane, blocking all traffic.

Once hopping out and locking the doors, he approached the house with caution as two husky men in black suits headed his way. Both looked like former MMA fighters, muscular builds, crooked noses, and calloused ears.

Without consent, the two bullies roughly frisked and patted Young Ham down to his socks. In search of a weapon he left under the Cadillac's front seat, once he briefly weighed the option of pulling up strapped like he was looking for trouble, but coming in packing would've said more wrong than it helped.

The heavy-handed twosome finished their shakedown and nodded to one another that he had come up clean. Young Ham smoothed out his clothes as he was escorted inside to meet the man responsible for setting things up.

Before he stepped a full two feet into the door, the hairs on the back of his neck stood straight, sensing something wasn't right.

He darted his eyes around the room and could feel the tension in the air, and could see it written on the faces of those present. There were about ten goons in suits and ties scattered about. Some standing. Others sat.

Poor Franco was in the middle.

Tied to a chair.

The Colombian drug lord's once-handsome face had been beaten into a bloody mess - almost unrecognizable. Thick yellowish fluid leaked from the crown of his head and dripped onto the snow-white carpet below. Judging by the uncontrolled shivers his banged-up body made, it was safe to say Franco had taken one hell of a thrashing.

"Young Ham, it is unfortunate we must meet like this," a voice said smoothly. "If not for various reasons that bring myself and my men to your country, you would've never seen or known I exist. My name is Ormiga but on American soil that means Ant."

"No disrespect, Ormiga - or Ant as you say," Young Ham replied, training his attention on the man seated in front of him. "But what does any of this have to do with me?"

He pointed at Franco, who hung on for dear life and barely had enough strength to lift his head.

Nodding in agreement, Ormiga continued.

"Yes, I understand how inconvenient it must be to enter a room full of armed men ready to blow off your head at the snap of my fingers. I ordered you here today because I want what belongs to me, and I will kill off everyone I think has something to do with stealing from me and my country."

Ormiga uncrossed his legs, stood to his feet, and walked over to Franco. He lifted his silk shirt for all to see and pulled a snub-nose .380 revolver from his trousers. Short breaths of air escaping Franco's lungs were the only tell-tale sign that he still had life in him.

Ormiga stuck the business end of the gun into Franco's mouth. Young Ham turned his head before the shot went off. When he faced forward again, Ormiga's piercing gray eyes - for the longest minute - searched his face for lies.

Having nothing to hide, Young Ham matched his stare, even while thinking he was next in line to have his cranium cracked like Franco. That is, until Ormiga released his eye grip, turned, and tossed the pistol to one of his soldiers - who caught it and exited without further notice.

"Please join me on a seat, Young Ham," Ormiga said, reclaiming his spot on the sofa and crossing his legs once again.

Ormiga's security team released their grips, and Young Ham accompanied him to the couch. He took a seat but not too close.

Within seconds, a cleanup crew hustled in and removed Franco's body, draping a large black trash bag over him and tying the drawstring tight in knots. And like that, Franco was stripped from sight.

"I am sorry. Now shall we continue? I do not like a thief - nor a liar. Bad combination. Both are bad for business. As you should know, cocaine brings money to my country. I love my country, and my country loves money. So when people steal my cocaine, they are taking money from my country."

Young Ham raised a hand to speak. "Ormiga, you still confuse me about why you called me here. I haven't stolen a crumb from nobody."

"I believe what you say. The eyes never lie. Unfortunately, Franco has sold you hundreds of stolen kilos from me and my people, and I want to know where the rest of it is."

"Once again, with all respect, it was never my business to know what Franco or anybody else had going on. All I do is spend my cash and keep it moving. No questions asked."

Ormiga raised an arm and summoned a man near. A tall, clean-shaven Colombian mob figure handed him a robust cigar.

As Ormiga lit it, Young Ham glanced at the shiny ring on his middle finger - then at the lighter in his hand.

A golden "M" was engraved on them both.

"Is there something wrong, Young Ham?" Ormiga asked, puffing and twisting the long stogie. "You look as though you seen a ghost."

"No, but I got-" Young Ham froze with his hand in his pocket. From every direction, guns cocked and aimed at him.

One false move and it was over.

Ormiga jumped to his feet and calmed everyone down. "It's okay… it's okay. What is it that you have, Young Ham?"

"I don't know what to make of this," he said carefully, "but I carry this wherever I go. It's the last thing I have to remind me of my Pop."

He removed from his pocket an identical lighter.

The room went still.

"Where in the world did you get that?" Ormiga asked incredulously. "My grandfather died of cancer years ago, and I was forced to overtake operations for Magnate-Rey's billion-dollar cocaine trade. This lighter was issued when I successfully trafficked five tons past U.S. Coast Guard patrol. Only elite smugglers are honored with this heirloom."

"That's deep," Young Ham admitted. "But when my Pop got knocked last year by the feds, I found this lighter, a hundred thousand in cash, and an addressed letter to me. Hidden inside a lamp at one of the houses he owned. Ironically, the note connected me to Franco, and that's when I started buying dope from him. This lighter is all I have left of the man that made me the hustler I am."

"For your father to possess the Magnate-Rey certificate," Ormiga said slowly, "then he must have known about my late grandfather. Which means he moved shiploads of Colombian product. Your father was nothing less than a made man. Therefore… if he was friend and business associate of Magnate-Rey, then my friend you are too."

Ormiga extended his hand.

Young Ham shook it firmly.

Outside, gasoline fumes crept into the air. Mafia men circled the mansion with gas cans, splashing flammable liquid along the exterior walls. Ormiga acted as if it were nothing.

"Young Ham, this will not be the last time you hear from me. I have eyes everywhere. Until then…" He smiled faintly. "Keep it real."

Both laughed but Young Ham took it serious.

As Young Ham hooked a left out of the mansion's circular driveway, flames licked the sky behind him. In the rearview mirror, the fire danced and swallowed what was left of Franco's last breath. Young Ham didn't blink. He drove steady but he wasn't alone.
Two houses down, parked beneath the shade of a dying oak tree, a blacked-out Tahoe sat idling. Inside, a pair of eyes tracked the Cadillac's movement through tinted glass.

"Yeah," the man in the passenger seat muttered, lowering a pair of binoculars. "That's him."

The driver adjusted his fitted cap and kept both hands on the steering wheel. "You sure?" he asked.

"I don't forget faces. Especially not that one."

The Tahoe remained still as Young Ham passed.

The passenger pulled out his phone and snapped a single picture through the windshield. Young Ham's CT-6 framed perfectly between smoke and fire.

He typed one message: Target confirmed.

The driver finally shifted the SUV into gear. They rolled off in the opposite direction, slow enough not to draw attention, fast enough not to lose time.

Up ahead, Young Ham checked his mirrors again. He recognized nothing unusual. Just traffic and the city. But something in his chest burned with curiosity. He reached into his pocket and felt the lighter.

The golden "M" pressed cold against his fingertips. Today had uncovered something bigger than business. He just didn't know how big.

I Found Me

Times had changed and were finally looking up for Lil Nate and his sister, Toya. After their mom, Jewel, came home from rehab cleaner than a whistle, Young Ham helped relocate them out of the projects. She found steady work and worked things out with the state to get her kids back.

Not only did Jewel put the pipe down and shake her habit, she seemed more caring and more mother-like than before.

About to turn sixteen in a few weeks, Lil Nate was excited about the promise Young Ham made to throw him a party at the Millennium - the spot for teenagers to really let loose. Young Ham always stood on his word, so Lil Nate was looking forward to it.

"Nate!" Toya called, poking her head into his room. "What you doing?"

She had grown fast. One look and you could tell she'd reached maturity early, making big brother overly protective.

"I was minding my business 'til you interrupted me," he said, eyeing her at the door. "And what I tell you about calling me Nate? I'm Chase. Get it right or take flight."

He grabbed a pillow and flung it her way.

Nowadays, being called Nate sounded corny. All school year he campaigned - friends and haters included - to address him by his middle name, Chase. He was fight-go-with-it serious about burying that first name. Only his homeboy Lil Larry had teasing privileges.

"Boy, ain't nobody trying to hear all that," Toya said, stepping over the pillow and walking all the way in. "I'm just checking on my big brother I looove so much."

"Cut it out, Toya," Chase said, unmoved. "Now what you want? 'Cause you not as slick as you think."

Toya rolled her eyes. "Can you call Young Ham and ask him to buy me the new J's that dropped yesterday? Pleaaase?"

"He just bought you some new shoes. Why you don't ask mama?"

"First off, Young Ham is a baller and mama is not. And if I had a cellphone like you, then I wouldn't need you to call him. Now would I, Einstein?"

She had a point.

"Dang, you be bugging," Chase muttered, grabbing his lucky headband. "I'll call him when we get back from the gym."

Chase waited for Lil Larry to get dropped off, then they planned to hit the courts and hustle two-on-two for cash. When the doorbell rang, Chase knew it could only be one person. He quickly blocked Toya from getting to it.

"What up, homie?" Chase said, opening the door.

Lil Larry stepped in wearing slides and gym shorts, still smelling like outside.

Despite his mom still running the streets getting high, the boy never let it break him. Some nights he slept at Chase's crib and went to school from there. They wore the same size, so whatever Chase had - he had too.

Following Chase's lead, Lil Larry switched his nickname to L. Said if his boy leveling up, he was too.

"Ain't nothing, my nigga," L said, standing six-foot-two and smiling wide. "Just glad I made it."

After they dapped it up, Chase closed and locked the door.

"Lil sis, where you headed?" L asked as Toya stepped out dressed and ready.

"Nowhere!" Chase said louder than normal. Thinking she hadn't spoken about going anywhere. Toya knew he wasn't with her just jumping up and leaving.

"To the store…daddy." Toya shot back.

"No, we going to the store," Chase corrected. "Then you going to the gym with us. And don't forget we ain't got no daddy, but we do got each other. That's all that counts."

"Since y'all taking me," Toya grinned, "y'all can buy my list of junk food. And I don't know why y'all always at the gym. Y'all ain't got nobody's game."

They laughed and stepped out.

The gym was crowded as usual. Inside, the air conditioning cooled everybody off, but the real action was outside under the shed-covered courts - where true ballers put up or shut up, running two-on-two for money.

Four teams were ready for battle. It was a single elimination, a hundred-dollar buy-in, and the winners took it all.

The first team to ten points won. No deuces. No threes. Every bucket counted as one. If you got skunked seven-nothing, you had to toss in another hundred because peter-roll was in effect.

Chase spotted two unfamiliar faces on one squad, but it didn't matter. They could get it like the rest.

He and L lost the free-throw shootout and had to sit the first game. It didn't last long. The new faces peter-rolled their opponents quick. Jackpot now sat at five hundred.

One of the new guys - later introduced as Quick - winked at Chase while walking off the court. Chase let the nonverbal call out slide.

When their turn came, Chase and L handled business and won 10-2, sending another squad home.

Now it was them versus the new boys. The losers stayed and watched. Secretly, hoping for Chase and L's defeat on behalf of the winnings they had taken home.

Chase matched up with Quick. Quick had a slight height advantage, but Chase prided himself on lockdown defense.

Game on.

He and L got the ball first. Chase attacked the rack twice, and L nailed a jump shot. They jumped out 3-0, but Quick answered.

Quick ripped Chase's pockets clean. From the sidelines you could hear the "oohs." Quick and his boy scored five unanswered points like it was a walk in the park. Toya folded her arms and watched quietly.

The Score 5-3. They were down.

L came down wrong on a rebound and sprained his ankle, but the game didn't stop for injuries. There were no excuses on the money court.

Chase tightened up, ripped Quick clean, and dished to L for a bucket. Back and forth they went.

The score 9-8. They lead.

Game point.

Toya cheered from her spot on the empty bench. "C'mon, Chase and L!"

Chase let L inbound. He posted up Quick, back to the basket. When L ran the fake pick, Chase spun baseline and elevated.

Quick fouled him hard and knocked him off balance. But not before Chase floated a no-look lob. L caught it with two hands and slammed it home.

"Game time!" L yelled, hanging on the rim.

Five hundred secured but Chase hit the ground mad. Mad that he had scraped up his knees and his lip was bleeding.

"Say, nigga," Chase growled, stepping toward Quick. "What's up with that dry fouling shit?"

"Fuck you," Quick shot back. "You ain't talking 'bout shit."

That was enough.

Chase launched first. He rushed Quick with a flurry of punches meant to end it. Quick folded fast. He had a run away mouth but no fight switch to catch up.

L snuck one in too. He touched up Quick's homeboy on general purposes. Toya ran on the court and jumped in, kicking and swinging like she'd been waiting on it. They had to pull her off.

On the walk home, Chase split the winnings. Two hundred for himself. Two hundred for L. One hundred for Toya.

"Toya," he laughed, shaking his head. "You crazy, girl. And you better not tell mama."

They were halfway down the block when the laughter faded and the adrenaline settled into something quieter.

Chase kept touching his lip, checking the swelling with his tongue while L replayed the alley-oop for the third time like it was destined for SportsCenter. Toya walked slightly ahead of them, clutching her folded hundred-dollar bill like it was a trophy.

"You ain't have to swing like that," L said, nudging Chase with his shoulder. "We already had the bread."

"He fouled me on purpose," Chase replied calmly.

"That wasn't basketball. That was hate."

L didn't argue.

What neither of them noticed was the dark sedan parked across from the corner store they had just passed, sitting too still for a neighborhood car.

Inside, a man scrolled through photos on his phone. One image showed Young Ham's CT-6 leaving a burning mansion. Another showed Chase mid-game at the court, body extended in the air as he lobbed the pass. The man zoomed in and out on Chase's face.

He turned the phone slightly so the driver could see. "That's him," he said quietly. "Same jawline."

The driver studied the picture of Chase, then switched to the photo of Young Ham standing outside Ormiga's mansion earlier that afternoon.

"Both are a match," the driver finally muttered.

The sedan remained parked as Chase, L, and Toya disappeared around the corner. The car eased off the curb without drawing attention and rolled in the opposite direction.

$ $ $ $ $

Later that evening, Young Ham sat alone at his kitchen island, staring at the lighter resting beside a half-finished glass of bourbon.

The golden "M" caught the reflection of the overhead lights, glowing faintly.

He hadn't told Monique what happened. Probably wouldn't. Not yet anyhow. But something inside felt off - like the threads of his life were getting pulled in opposite directions.

And maybe they were.

Because he had no idea that somewhere in the city, someone had already circled his name.

New Boss, Same Rules

"Toast to the CKC players! These boys been hustling and making moves since they were in baby shoes!"

DJ Fiz's voice boomed over Majestics, the fully nude strip club buzzing with money and ego. The crowd roared as the Cash Keepers stood one by one, bottles of Dom Pérignon raised high while the DJ shouted out top authority cliques in the building. Bills rained down from every direction, tiling the floor in cash like confetti.

After the shot-out, dancers flooded their section, putting on a private show that was less about performance and more about the dollars falling from the ceiling.

Youngin's cousin, Big Zeke, celebrated with the crew. Though he was originally from the -21 Thurgood neighborhood, he had been loyal and getting it in with them for some time. He had even dropped a hundred thousand on a custom CKC diamond piece and chain - heavy enough to put a crook in your neck.

"What's on your mind, big man?" Young Ham asked, sliding next to him. "You haven't taken a swig or slapped an ass cheek the whole night."

Big Zeke half-smiled, still scanning the room. He pulled his weight in upper-class hustling but mostly operated as their chief enforcer, eyes always moving.

"I'm good, boss. Just making sure we straight in here. Plus, I smoke more than I drink water. Know what I'm saying?"

Smiley leaned in and nudged Young Ham's arm. "Look at this crazy nigga Youngin', always wanting attention."

Young Ham barely reacted. His mind drifted elsewhere - past the dancers, past the celebration, and past Youngin' getting cheers behind standing on the bar top and throwing wads of cash.

A week had passed since Franco's brain splattered across white carpet, and still no word from Ormiga.

Plies' "Shawty" shook the speakers and boosted the energy. Then she appeared out of nowhere.

A yellow-bone with ocean-green eyes that locked directly on Young Ham moved through the crowd like she had a destination. She worked her way closer with seductive control, drawing attention from everyone - except the only man she was aiming for.

When she got within touching distance, Big Zeke stepped in front of her, palm raised.

"Slow your roll, lil mama. You know my nigga or something?"

Her expression didn't flinch. "I didn't get paid to answer questions, sweety. Only to give the king of the Bricks a message. Now if you'll let me pass."

Big Zeke hated a woman with a slick mouth, but he looked back at Young Ham for instruction. Young Ham gave a slight nod, and Big Zeke stepped aside.

She moved forward with the confidence of someone who knew the effect she had. Dropping to her knees in front of Young Ham, she made her presence impossible to ignore. Her tongue ring caught the light as she leaned in, dragging her heated tongue against his denim shorts.

But Young Ham wasn't focused on the performance. He took a closer look at the jewelry in her mouth, recognition flickering in his eyes.

A golden M.

With a subtle wink, she rose and headed toward the club's exclusive private rooms. Security didn't ask questions when Young Ham followed her beyond the velvet ropes.

The hallway was dim, quiet, and removed from the chaos outside. She disappeared around a corner, and when Young Ham reached the cracked door she slipped into, he stepped inside.

Two men stood waiting, arms relaxed but ready. Both were handpicked Colombians from Ormiga's organization.

"Welcome aboard, Young Ham," the slick-haired one began calmly. "Ormiga sends his greetings with respect. We are here to inform you of the arrangements on behalf of the Magnate-Rey industry. You will comply with all instructions throughout this relationship. The terms are non-negotiable. That means you play by our rules."

The second man remained silent behind dark shades. A sealed manila envelope was placed in Young Ham's hand.

"Our roving team will ensure your package arrives safely," the spokesman continued. "You will orchestrate the pickup. There cannot be mishaps when millions of dollars' worth of product is involved. Forget Franco. We do not operate under his guidelines. You are a wise young man. Remain that way."

They left without waiting for a response.

Young Ham stayed still for a moment, weighing the envelope in his hand like it carried more than paper. Then the door opened again. Green eyes reentered and closed it behind her.

"Handsome," she said softly, stepping closer. "Your service has been paid for."

$ $ $ $ $

Later that night, when Young Ham returned home, Monique was fresh from the shower, wrapped in nothing but a towel. A true crime documentary played in the background as she ran her nightly routine - studying, and strengthening the discipline that came with chasing real goals.

"Hey, Moni," he said, sitting at the edge of the bed. "How was your day?"

"Busy and boring," she replied with a sigh. "I was probably on my feet all day, ripping and running. I swear if I don't get help soon,

I'm going to pass out."

"Not before you die from a Law & Order overdose," he teased, rubbing her foot gently.

"Hmm. Just what I needed. And what have you been doing all day to where my calls went unanswered? Don't let me find out."

He had forgotten to call her back.

"Chill out, Moni. We been rocking too long for all that. I was busy...my bad."

"Boy, I'm playing." she shot back.

She paused, then flipped the conversation. "I might have something big on the table. I got a call about possibly working on a classified case the FBI been building on for months. Could be the opportunity I've been praying for."

"You know I got your back," he said, studying her carefully. "Just don't come shaking me down."

But later, as he lay awake beside her, the truth pressed him. It was going to be a hard pill to swallow, but she needed to know what he represented in the streets. Monique would either have to accept the life he had stepped fully into, or pack her bags and leave. Because when this level of the game hits the fan, there's no such thing as halfway.

Game Time

Chase and L were upstairs playing Call of Duty, killing time while waiting on supper. Once again, Josephine had pulled a disappearing act, leaving her son crashing at Jewel's house for nearly a week without even swinging by to ask if it was okay. It wasn't the first time she'd done it, and Jewel had tolerated it before, but this time felt different.

Jewel understood struggle. She had lived it. But watching her longtime friend spiral back into the same destructive cycle hit deeper now that she had fought her way clean. She wasn't upset about L staying over, she loved that boy like one of her own. It was the principle. The repeated neglect. The destructive pattern she hadn't spotted while on her own dope trip.

After dinner, the boys were back on the PS3 when the doorbell rang. A moment later, raised voices broke through the house. Their mothers were downstairs arguing, at each other's throat with raw emotions. Chase and L paused the game and rushed to the stairwell.

"Larry, get your stuff and let's go. Now," Josephine snapped the moment her son appeared.

L stood still for a second, shoulders tight.

He had grown up hard. He took the good with the bad and faced life however it came, but in moments like this, Chase could read the hurt in his homie's eyes. It wasn't anger. It was disappointment dressed up as toughness.

"Jose, I meant what I said," Jewel responded firmly. "That boy ain't going nowhere with you until you clean yourself up like I had to do to get mine back."

Jewel stood grounded in her truth. She had been clean over a year - off the streets, off alcohol, off drugs. She had put her weight back on, kept herself together, and rebuilt what she once tore down. Holding back tears, she showed tough love to the friend she had known for two decades.

"You're one of the few friends I got, Jose," Jewel continued, voice shaking but steady. "But I refuse to sit back and watch them people take that boy like they almost did mine. Over my dead body he ain't walking out with you tonight. Get yourself some help. And if you try to call the law, I'll personally show them your arms and let them know everything you been doing. I love you like a sister, but before he go back under your roof, and deal with your mess. I'll let them white folks find him a better place."

Silence stretched between them.

Josephine's pride flared, but even she knew Jewel wasn't wrong. She turned on her heels and disappeared into the night.

The next day...
Chase and L sat in the room, the tension from the night before still hanging heavy. Chase had just hung up with a cheerleader from their SSA league's Stars Squad. They were waiting for the next round of the tournament to start up. Winning the championship meant exposure. Real scouts and real opportunities from elite colleges.

A handful of NBA players had once dribbled in that same academy league. If they made the all-star game in Baltimore, doors could open. Chances of playing for Duke and Kentucky, the big programs, shot to the roof just for being on the court.

"Bro, you over there looking like somebody stole your girl," Chase joked, tossing his phone on the bed.

"Nah, kinfolk," L replied, rubbing his head slowly. "That shit last night messed me up. I always knew T-Jones was cracked out, and only gave a damn when it was check time. But bump that. I'm tired of losing in life, bro. Tired of being broke and unhappy. A nigga wanna have money and do what he want."

Chase leaned back against the wall. "I feel you, but we gotta be patient. A dreamer can't stop dreaming. This ball gon' bring cash, plus recognition. We just gotta stay at it."

"Patience the best friend of broke," L shot back, lowering his voice when he realized where they were. "I'm just being real. I'm sick of living in dreamland while reality keeps slapping me. Screw basketball and hard work. This gon' bring cash if we stay at it?"

Then he reached into his pocket and pulled out a fat crack sack. He waved it in front of Chase's face like a flag.

Chase jumped up instantly. "What you doing, L? Where you get that?"

"Relax before you have a stroke," L said, grinning. "This what got Young Ham on swole. I been messing with Big Zeke, who rock with Youngin', and they both Cash Keepers."

The room went quiet.

"So you been hustling behind my back?" Chase asked, betrayal cutting through his voice. "When we supposed to be thicker than blood?"

"I'm telling you now," L replied. "I didn't know how to bring it up because you always stressing about going to the league. But bump that. I want mines now."

Chase didn't respond right away.

Deep down, he couldn't deny the game's pull. He had watched Young Ham grow taller in the lifestyle, and the way people moved when he entered a room, had planted seeds inside him that basketball didn't water fast enough.

"Man, I ain't gon' lie," Chase admitted finally. "Sometimes I be thinking about that good life. Who really make it from the hood to the NBA anyway? Nobody I know."

"Exactly," L said. "How much money you got?"

"Close to four hundred. Why?"

"After I sell this little bit I got, we can go in together on something bigger."

"Where we gon' sell it?" Chase asked cautiously. "I'm trying to get paid, not delayed."

"The Bricks," L answered without hesitation.

Chase shook his head. "Young Ham and the Cash Keepers got that locked down twenty-four hours. They smoke fools trying to make a move on their turf."

L's eyes hardened. "If we gon' worry about where we can and can't get money, we might as well stay dribbling a ball. Entering the game like signing up for the Army. You never know who you might go to war with."

Back in the Lab

"Girls, we've entered a new realm of the game," Young Ham said, laying the envelope's contents out on the table as Adiva, Kenya, and Queen leaned in. "With that comes new responsibilities. Stay extra careful when you're feeling out your surroundings. Listen to your body. Don't lock eyes with nobody longer than necessary when you're in the field."

Inside the sealed envelope were the date, time, and location to retrieve a vehicle loaded with three hundred kilos. A second sheet outlined manufacturing breakdowns that even forced Young Ham to reread it several times before it fully clicked. This wasn't Franco-level hustle.

This was industrial.

As Young Ham broke it down step by step, the Nigerian trio gave him their undivided attention. Their beauty disguised ruthlessness. Their education disguised intent. Over the years they had grown immune to violence and corruption, and were trained to move without emotion when the mission called for it.

It wasn't just loyalty that bound them to Young Ham. It was belief.

"New boss, same rules," Adiva said calmly. "Let's get it."

Adiva led the pack now, not just in experience but in composure. Since aligning as one of Young Ham's top lieutenants, she had absorbed layers of the game and reshaped it in her own way, mentoring Kenya and Queen with the same discipline.

They were no longer cramped in a small apartment. The trio now lived in a paid-for three-bedroom, two-car garage home. It looked modest on the outside, but was lavishly decked out within. Their cultural backgrounds defied chasing luxury just for show. They valued the fruits of their labor, but more than anything family came first.

After briefing them, Young Ham hugged each one before stepping out.

$ $ $ $ $

"What is taking the department so long to build a solid case against this low-life? We should've already had him behind bars snitching like they all do when it's time to pay the piper." DEA Special Agent Randy Cummings said, jaw tight.

The conference room went quiet.

Randy had spent over twenty years inside the Department of Justice, chasing international traffickers and dismantling syndicates. He was in his late forties, disciplined build, and had a relentless appetite for capturing bad guys. But beneath it all, fatigue had started settling into his bones.

Assistant Special Agent Natasha Woods sat poised across the table. She was twenty-eight years old, and darker than licorice. Each day she hated being in her own skin. She talked, lived, and acted as though she was anything but Black.

Natasha's hatred for her own grew from being abandoned as a baby. On a rainy day, she was found on the front steps of the Fire Department, and later adopted by Caucasian parents.

"Agent Cummings," she began professionally, "we've repeatedly come up short on direct linkage to Foreal Hamilton Jr., aka Young Ham. He's shown to be clean on surface-level transactions. We've prioritized tying him to large shipments of cocaine and to the March homicide of Shavanz Booker. We're now working with a private investigative firm to establish deeper financial patterns that could justify a federal takedown."

Randy exhaled sharply. "I don't care how you do it. I want him behind bars before he takes his next shit or breathes easy again."

The room stiffened when Randy slammed down a closed fist, startling everyone except Natasha. His retirement was approaching, and whether he secured a victory on Young Ham or not, his pension would clear the same.

Natasha's motivation was different. She saw Young Ham as her stepping stone - the case that could elevate her career once Randy stepped down.

"Point of information, sir," Natasha said, all eyes cutting her way. "We're currently using our computer tracking and auxiliary data records to show a pattern of criminal intent."

Randy held back on blasting Natasha openly, for wasting his time and saying a bunch of nothing.

"Swell, then let's hit our target the first time. I don't like my food cold."

He dismissed the group with a hand wave. But once the meeting adjourned and the door shut behind the last agent, Randy lingered.

"Ms. Woods," he said quietly, "your diligence will only take you so far in this department."

He stood close enough to where Natasha tasted his cheap cologne. She held his gaze, reading his lustful expression. Power was currency in that building, just like money on the streets. And she intended to spend it wisely.

"Sir, you know how hard I work at proving my worth." She said, sensing how bad he wanted her.

Secretly, for the past three months, they involved themselves in sexual interactions. Even though Randy was a racist dick-head. He had an untamable love for nectar, a darker shade of brown.

"How about proving your worth right now, and I'll see about mentioning your name as my successor."

He lifted her tight- fitting mini skirt and squeezed. Her petite frame made it easy for him to place her on top of the oak-stained desk. In one motion, Randy moved Natasha's panties aside while freeing his member, and ramming it inside her warm flesh.

They humped vigorously. His short strokes had Natasha moaning. People were outside so she panted low. She had climbed too far to be knocked down. When Randy stopped and backed out of her. She slid off the desk and onto her knees.

Her deep throat tactics had the old man's eyes rolling to the back of his head, blowing his mind. He palmed her head, pinched together her nostrils, and shoved himself forcefully.

Natasha wasn't the one for tapping out. She took all he had with a wink and smile, no gagging. He buckled at the knees, unable to hold back any longer. She stayed until the last drop, then straightened her hair, wiped her mouth, and whisked out of the door.

$ $ $ $ $

Adiva decided that Queen was getting behind the wheel, and driving away in the parked vehicle. Kenya was given the "crash and burn" mission, meaning she'd sacrifice herself if police arrived unexpectedly. Adiva would be on standby if either of them needed a way out.

If everything went according to plan, the contraband-loaded vehicle would be transferred to a low-key spot outside the city where packaging and storage were the only activity.

Queen bent the block first in a 2002 Chevy Impala, cruising past the white mini-van parked in front of a brown brick home with a trimmed lawn. Less than ten minutes later, Kenya looped back in a Ford F-150, scanning for any hint of unmarked surveillance.

Young Ham had trained them to trust their instincts. The body always gave warnings before the mind caught up.

Five minutes later, Adiva drove through casually, eyes forward, playing it like she was just passing by. She turned onto the main road, pulled into a convenience store parking lot, and texted: GIHYL.

Get It How You Live.

Fuck them other niggas 'cause I ride for my niggas. Kenya was crunk when she got the text from Adiva. She turned down the music, and prepared mentally. She came ready whenever the heat went down, and her guns burst first anytime there was smoke.

She stood five-foot-five with the heart of a lion, and measurements of what street dudes called a quarter-horse. But she was gay.

"Fuck them other bitches 'cause I'm down for my bitches. I'll ride for my bitches. Fuck them other bitches!" She bounced to the melody in her head, and waited for her next instructions.

Queen glanced at the text, and smirked. She parked a few streets down, dressed in neutral athletic gear - sports bra, tights, light sneakers. She jogged casually down the block like she belonged there, slowing near the mini-van's bumper as if adjusting her shoe. In one fluid motion, she raised up wearing black gloves, did a quick scan down the block, then opened the unlocked door and slid behind the wheel.

Under the driver's seat, her fingers brushed cold metal. Keys. She brought the engine to life and pulled off smoothly, merging into traffic without drawing attention.

Adiva fell in behind at a measured distance, close enough to block interruption but far enough not to look attached. Kenya trailed the Buick at a three-car cushion, keeping her eyes locked in the rearview. They moved as one organism.

The drive to the safe house went without incident. A few stop signs here, two traffic lights there, then the highway. When the van signaled and turned into the cul-de-sac drop location, the mission was already complete.

Adiva peeled off in one direction, and Kenya traveled in another.

The Streets Are Calling

"Man, I feel like Tony Montana with all this dope around me," Smiley said, stacking another ready-made brick against the living room wall inside the safe house.

It was three in the morning, and the Cash Keepers were wide awake, compressing blocks of cocaine like it was a factory line instead of a trap house.

"Crack I ain't never smoked," Youngin' muttered, waving his hand through the air, "but I think I just caught a contact off this."

"That's why I told y'all to bring masks," Big Zeke said, shaking his head.

"Nah," Youngin' shot back, grinning. "What I remember you saying was you was gon' bring the masks."

"Kinfolk, you been hard of hearing since we was kids. Remember all them ass whoopings you caught?"

"Man, fuck you," Youngin' laughed.

The purity of the cocaine was unlike anything they had touched before. It gave them room to shave off a quarter kilo and still stretch the rest without weakening the product. Step by step, they followed the handwritten instructions Ormiga had provided on converting it to Grade A street-ready weight.

By the time the final rectangle was wrapped, greased, taped, and weighed, the original three hundred kilos had grown into four hundred large.

It was their biggest score yet.

"So they really smoked Franco?" Youngin' asked quietly.

Young Ham paused at that.

Franco had kept it solid from day one. Whatever went wrong, it wasn't whispered freely. But Young Ham knew one thing - when money stacks high enough, loyalty starts folding under its own weight.

"That's the price when relationships get contaminated by greed," Young Ham said evenly. "At the end of the day, we all chasing a piece of paper called money."

$ $ $ $ $

"Y'all be careful sellin' that rock out here," an old smoker with no teeth warned. "This Cash Keepers' block."

Chase and L had taken the bus to the eastside earlier and were now hitting licks in the Bricks like they owned the pavement. Some fiends turned their noses up at outsiders moving work without permission. Others didn't care - dope was dope, and if it hit right, coming off their money was no problem.

"Yeah, yeah, we hear you," Chase said. "But this our hood too."

The old smoker limped closer.

"I ain't tellin' you what to do. I'm just tellin' you what to expect. They call me J. I been runnin' these streets since y'all was in diapers. It ain't always about you and yours. Having people is worth more than having money. You'll learn that soon enough."

"Why you walk with that limp?" L asked bluntly.

Dopefiend J chuckled.

"That's a war wound from a lifetime ago. I regret how much of my life turned out. Wish I'd took bein' a father serious instead of fallin' in love with this glass pipe. But that's another story."

He looked at Chase.

"Since I like y'all, I'll bring y'all all the traffic. Keep me high, and you ain't gotta chase nobody down."

"That's a bet," L said, breaking off a small piece and handing it over.

Dopefiend J backed up his words and delivered, lick after lick until their sack ran dry. You could tell Dopefiend J had a strong hustle before he flipped into a smoker. When the money was counted, Chase leaned back.

"So what we gettin' into now?"

"What you mean," L said. "We goin' up the hill to holler at Big Zeke."

"Hold up. You said Big Zeke a Cash Keeper, right?" Chase asked. "Man, he gon' call Young Ham on me."

"Chill, bro." L smiled. "He don't know you like that. I'ma do the talking anyway."

Big Zeke cracked open apartment door 702, smoke drifting out behind him.

"Tell me somethin' good, lil homies."

"We tryna grab a circle," L said.

"You got six?"

Six hundred was counted dollar for dollar and passed through the torn screen. Big Zeke flipped through it quick, disappeared, then returned with a tight circular ounce in a sandwich bag.

"Where y'all from anyway?"

"Right here in the Bricks. O2 on ours."

Big Zeke laughed and shut the door.

Big Al's store had been around since Young Ham used to walk Chase and his sister inside for candy. The memory sat in the background whether Chase wanted it there or not. Dopefiend J was shoplifting a .40 ounce of Old E when they entered.

"Youngsters, y'all missin' money left and right," Dopefiend J called from the back. "Better grab it while it's hot."

Chase noticed the way Dopefiend J gravitated toward him, seeming a little too eager with helping out. But hustle was hustle, and Dopefiend J had enough to go around.

"We need somewhere to chop this up," Chase said.

"Roll with me," Dopefiend J answered. "I got y'all."

They grabbed a single razor and a box of sandwich bags before following him across the street to the elderly building section of the projects.

"This where the gangster granny stay," Dopefiend J said proudly. "She don't smoke. Don't mess with none of that. But she solid for the hood."

Knock. Knock.

"Ms. Marlene, it's J."

The locks twisted one by one before the door cracked open. An orange cat darted out. "That dang cat crazy as these fools," she muttered.

Dopefiend J stepped forward.

"Ms. Marlene, me and my nephews just need to get off the block for a minute. Laws hot."

"Child, I ain't ask no questions," she said, rolling aside. "Just don't bring no trouble."

Ms. Marlene gave Chase a once over.

"Nephew! This boy here could pass for your son if you ask me."

"What about yo cat?" Chase asked, closing the door behind him.

"He ran his tail out there, so that's where he wanna be. He knows where I stay."

Inside, the walls were covered with faded Polaroids of family and friends, memories of a life that existed before these new buildings replaced the old ones. Ms. Marlene had done everything in the projects, but left.

Dopefiend J led them to the back room, grabbed a hardback book from off the dresser, and nodded. Chase and L chose to hold up the walls.

"Watch and learn, youngins. Let me show both y'all how I used to get down when I was at my best."

L handed Dopefiend J the blade and work. He chopped the ounce down with practiced hands. His precise cutting rounded out eighty-eight stones, no crumbs to show.

"Before this pipe got me," Dopefiend J said quietly, "they called me pop-a-rock 'cause I could bust a rock down with my fingernail. This life ain't for the weak. It takes more than it gives."

Chase listened.

"It cost me my two boys that I never raised because I was too ashamed. So I stayed away and sunk deeper."

"Why you ain't quit?" he asked.

Dopefiend J stared at the floor.

"When you trapped in addiction, it ain't that simple. I'm tellin' you this 'cause I was y'all age once. Know when to say enough. If you don't, this game gon' take more than you bargained for."

The warning hung in the room heavier than the product on the table.

Outside, sirens wailed somewhere in the distance. And for a split second, Chase felt something he hadn't felt before.

Doubt.

Pick a Side

Monique bounced in her seat, singing along to her favorite Keyshia Cole song as she drove downtown. The morning had unfolded perfectly. Hair done. Nails fresh. Outfit pressed. She looked every bit the woman who belonged in a federal building, and today was going to be a breakthrough like never before.

Though she lacked experience on high-profile cases, she knew that if she delivered something concrete, it could reshape her portfolio overnight. She told herself she had nothing to worry about. As long as she trusted her instincts, she'd find something useful against her assigned target.

But deep down, she also understood that working alongside federal investigators carried risk. Law enforcement officials, and those close to them, were often targets of retaliation.

Still, she double checked her appearance, then stepped into the building steadily. Natasha Woods greeted her with a firm handshake.

"Ms. Thorton, I'm glad you could make it."

Monique followed her into a small but cozy office space, decorated with awards, framed photos with white girls, and stacks of case files. Natasha moved with authority, flipping through a folder filled with surveillance photos: cars, jewelry, properties, clubs, money trails, and faces connected through invisible lines.

"So, was finding our building complicated?" Natasha asked. "A lot of folks get lost."

"No, actually the directions off my GPS worked everything out."

"Good, so let me start by saying that we've been tracking this network for over a year," Natasha explained. "These individuals are connected to large cash transactions, untaxed millions, and control East Austin's distribution routes. A bunch of organized thugs is what I call them."

She paused, sliding one final folder across the desk.

"And this," she said quietly, "is the masterminded ringleader."

Monique's breath was caught in her throat.

Young Ham's face stared back at her from a printed image. Her stomach dropped. This was the man she loved. The man she trusted. The man she slept beside.

"This can't be real," she whispered to herself.

But federal agencies did not build cases on guesses. If he was on their radar, something big on the lawbreaking side was in motion.

"Ms. Thorton," Natasha observed carefully, reading her reaction. "Are you alright?"

Monique forced composure.

"I'm fine. May I use the restroom for a moment?"

She barely made it to the ladies' room before the weight of it hit her. She locked the stall door and pressed her hands against the cool tile wall, fighting tears.

Get yourself together.

You're stronger than this.

She rinsed her face, checked her reflection, and steadied her breathing before returning.

Natasha gave her a look of disgust but resumed without hesitation.

"This individual goes by Young Ham. He has controlled significant narcotics activity in East Austin for roughly two years. His father was a known figure in the same arena. We believe the son has expanded operations beyond what his father ever achieved."

Each word felt like a blade.

"We brought you in," Natasha continued, "because our superiors believe you can help fill the missing pieces. Not only to prosecute Mr. Hamilton, but to dismantle the rest of his posse poisoning these neighborhoods."

Why they wanted her involvement was clear. They wanted her dark skinned enough to blend in where whites couldn't, and streetwise enough to get close and gather information.

Monique sat there, torn in half. Everything she had heard clashed against the man she knew. The tenderness of his touch, and the life he promised her. But if the evidence was real…Then what?

Later, she left the federal building carrying a briefcase of documents that could imprison the man she loved. Instead of going home, she merged onto I-35 and checked into a hotel for the night.

She needed space. She needed clarity. And for the first time, she wasn't sure which side of the line she stood on.

This What I Do

Young Ham tiptoed into the house a little after midnight, expecting Monique to be curled beneath the sheets, fast asleep like usual. Instead, he found the bed neatly made.

Too neat.

Her side was untouched, and her tablet blinked on the nightstand with an unread message.

He picked it up and sat on the edge of the mattress, wondering why his close-at-heart companion wasn't under the covers. The moment he opened the message and started reading, he felt it in his gut. Nothing good ever started with silence like this.

And as his eyes moved across the screen, he knew the days of deception had finally caught up with him.

Foreal, or should I say Young Ham,

I can't begin to understand all the lies you've managed to cover up this past year we've known each other. Leaving you wasn't easy. But I can't keep living in a house built on secrets. I never told you this before because I didn't want to relive it, but growing up, I watched my daddy choose that same lifestyle over us. I saw what it did to my mother. I saw what it did to our family. Before I lose myself loving a man who chooses the streets over peace, I'd rather walk away now than break later. Please don't make this harder by coming to look for me.

Always wishing you the best,
Monique.

Young Ham lowered the tablet slowly and looked around the bedroom for the first time. It felt different.

Empty.

Monique's walk-in closet stood open, cleaned out completely. No heels lined up against the wall. No colorful dresses hanging. No faint scent of her perfume lingering in the air. It was like she had erased herself.

She was a real one.

When he got shot and lay in the hospital wrapped in bandages, she stayed at his bedside day and night. When he got transferred to the county and fought that nine-month court battle, she never wavered. Even after he bonded out on a hundred-thousand-dollar bail, she cooked for him, took care of him, and stood solid while he moved through the motions of business.

She loved him without hesitation.

The thought of losing her companionship hit his chest like a hammer.

He exhaled heavy, feeling stupid. He really thought he could keep his dealings sealed off in one world and not expect his live-in girlfriend to eventually discover who he truly was behind the mask.

He had always planned to tell her.

One day.

Break it down from the beginning. Explain how he built the empire, lived a crime-filled life, and avoided the law daily. How it started small and grew bigger than he imagined. He just needed time to set it up right.

Now she was gone.

And she'd found out on her own.

Getting her back was all that mattered. He'd do whatever it took. But for now, he'd respect her wishes. Even though everything in him wanted to tear through the city searching for her just to look her in the eyes and apologize.

$ $ $ $ $

Days passed.

The chances of Monique rethinking her decision and walking back through that door grew slimmer by the hour. Instead of sitting around long-faced, Young Ham poured himself back into the hustle.

Bringing Big Zeke into the fold proved invaluable. The Cash Keepers now had another foothold outside Texas. Big Zeke's Utah relative- Kidd, the young and buzzing artist out west - gave them leverage in places nobody expected.

After performing at South by Southwest, Kidd rocked the stage, then boarded a Greyhound bus back home carrying more than just luggage. Tucked away was a brick of Texas' finest.

Kidd and his Mountain Gang Crew jumped at Big Zeke's offer, pooling ninety thousand in cash for five bricks at eighteen a block during a drought that had prices climbing. It was a deal too sweet for any hustler's refusal.

Soon, they were moving no less than thirty kilos at a time whenever they tapped Big Zeke's line. His monthly flip climbed to fifty, sometimes sixty kilos. He was quiet, efficient, and expanding.

Smiley tightened routes through Louisiana, Alabama, and Mississippi. He only touched down every third Sunday - their coded "game day." That meant a heavy shipment had arrived safe. Smiley drove in town unannounced, secured his cut, then disappeared just as quietly as he came.

Business was booming.

But inside the circle, cracks were forming.

Out of the crew, Youngin' loved the spotlight too much. He owned a fleet of flashy cars, and camped inside strip clubs throwing money in broad daylight like cameras didn't exist.

Too many times his reckless mouth sparked unnecessary tension with other hustlers who felt disrespected. Young Ham had to step in more than once. Pop had always warned him about the ones closest to you being the ones that could break you.

Youngin' moved weight flawlessly. His trafficking skills were clean and incomparable. He shifted products from one hand to another with precision, and stacked paper naturally.

But discipline?

That was another story.

"Youngin', you gotta tighten up," Young Ham stressed after another near-incident at the club. "This ain't just about you. We tied together. If you fall, we all fall."

Youngin' nodded, but pride still flickered behind his eyes.

"I got you, Brick. I'm chill. Dude was just talking sideways."

Young Ham studied him for a second longer. Because empires don't usually collapse from outside pressure.

They crumble from within.

In Between Worlds

The hotel room felt unfamiliar. Monique sat on the edge of the bed, still dressed, staring at the beige walls like they might answer something for her. The city lights bled through the curtains, but even that outside glow felt distant.

She hadn't broken down since leaving the federal building. Not in the car. Not at check-in. Not even when she closed the hotel door behind her. But now…it settled in.

Mastermind.

Distribution routes.

Untaxed millions.

East Austin narcotics activity.

She replayed Natasha's words in her head. How she described him didn't sound like the man who rubbed her feet after long days. That didn't sound like the man who held her at night. But love had blinded women before.

She stood and studied her reflection in the mirror. "Were you really this naïve?" she mumbled under her breath.

Her daddy used to come home reeking of liquor and lies. She remembered her mother sitting at the kitchen table pretending everything was fine for the neighbors. Pretending the lights weren't about to get cut off. Pretending the cops weren't patrolling the block more often than usual.

Monique swore she would never be a woman sitting in a house pretending not to see the obvious. Yet here she was. Living in a man's world without asking enough questions.

She moved toward the window and pulled the curtain back. Cars passed below, unaware of the war going on inside her chest.

One side said: He loves you. He needs you. He would never hurt you intentionally.

The other side said: You've seen this before. You know how this ends. You know what happens when a woman stands beside a man who chooses the streets.

Her phone buzzed and made her heart jump. For half a second, she hoped it was him but it wasn't. Just a message from work confirming the follow-up meeting. Meaning they expected her to continue getting closer, then report back to them.

Her chest tightened.

She sat back down on the bed and pressed her hands against her temples. If she cooperated, she would be the reason he fell. If she refused, she risked losing her career - maybe worse.

"What did you do, Young Ham?" she whispered.

She thought about the nights he came home late but still made time to ask about her day. The way he zoned out sometimes when money conversations got too detailed. The sudden cash sprout and coded calls he brushed off as "business."

The signs had been there all along. She just chose to ignore them. A tear slipped down her cheek. Not because the feds labeled him a kingpin, but because she still loved him. And loving him made this harder than walking away ever would.

She reached for her phone and hovered her thumb over his name. One call. That's all it would take. But if she called him, he'd weaken her. And she couldn't afford to be weak.

Not now.

She locked the phone and set it face down on the nightstand.

For the first time in a long time, Monique felt like she was standing in between two worlds at once. The world she built with Young Ham, and the world that demanded she choose who she really was. Time wasn't on her side.

And meeting with the feds was coming fast.

WANNA BE A BALLER

The Millennium was jam-packed. Young Ham had dropped a serious grip to rent the entire building for the day. Every game, every movie screen, every slice of pizza and soda inside the complex was prepaid and open to the public. If you walked in, you ate. If you played, it was on him.

He'd popped up at the crib early that morning while they were still asleep and took all three of them to Active Athlete. He splurged a stack close to a grand on each of them. Whatever gear they grabbed, whatever kicks they laced up, he nodded and told the cashier to ring it. Today wasn't about money. It was about memories.

Since Chase was the man of the hour, Young Ham doubled back after the shoe store and walked him into Goldmine Jewelers. Chase picked out a solid 24k rope chain. Then the unthinkable happened when Young Ham paid to have a 2.5-carat diamond stud pierced into Chase's left ear.

"When y'all make it to the league," Young Ham laughed, "I want all my money back... plus interest."

Toya rode shotgun in the truck so Young Ham missed Chase and L's exchange when he made the comment about them entering the league. Young Ham talked about one day watching them suit up for the Spurs, his favorite team, and hearing their names echo in the arena.

He was going to be hotter than fish grease when he found out Chase and L had hoop dreams of balling in the d-league, as in dope.

Things were going smooth inside the Millennium until Toya drifted into the arcade section. She locked eyes with a stranger who mistook her for somebody else. The boy stepped wrong, and grabbed Toya where he shouldn't have.

Chase and L went at it hard in the shoot-a-round game. L looked over his shoulder and spotted Toya arguing with some dude in her face. He dropped the mini basketball, and tapped Chase's arm.

"Ugly ass nigga!" Toya yelled. "I don't play that shit."

Chase and L parted the small crowd that had formed around the drama, getting between Toya and the stranger.

"Calm down, Toya, and tell me what happened." Chase said.

Toya's rage had grown since foster care. She resented men of all ages, the very cause of her inability to have kids.

"You want me to calm down after this punk ass nigga grabbed my ass."

Chase and L's head snapped. Toya at fifteen had a body that caused young and old men to stare.

"Yo playboy." Chase said calmly. "Please say you didn't disrespect my sister at my birthday party."

Before he could deny the charges brought against him, L had already shoved him. Chase followed with a straight punch that sent him stumbling into a gaming machine. Toya wasn't backing down either. She jumped in swinging, landing kicks of fury that had been building longer than that moment.

Security was radioed and rushed in breaking up the melee. The three of them were escorted to the back office, adrenaline still running hot. The flashlight cop asked questions but didn't get much out of no one.

"Okay, who's coming to get you three?" the security guard asked.

Chase didn't hesitate. " My cousin Young Ham gon' come get us."

In the Escalade, Young Ham drove in silence. No music. No small talk. Chase already knew Young Ham felt unappreciated. He learned early that the big homie was a thinker, and those around him would become thinkers too.

"You can't move like that," Young Ham said, eyes forward, voice controlled but firm. "Y'all think I'ma always be around to clean it up but y'all gotta learn to walk light."

"He grabbed my sister," Chase snapped.

"Toya can handle herself," Young Ham shot back. "Y'all gon' mess around and flush everything y'all done on the court."

Chase's voice cracked. "Man, forget college ball. I'm ready to get paper in these streets like you."

That one hit. Young Ham's grip tightened on the steering wheel.

"Being like me ain't what's up," he said low. "Y'all see the shine. You don't see the price."

Chase remembered the night crackhead Jimbo broke into their apartment. The night Toya was hurt. The night Young Ham showed up and made sure it never happened again. He'd never thanked him properly. Didn't know how.

"Be better than me," Young Ham continued. "That's the only way this mean something."

"No lie, Young Ham," L interrupted. "I'm ready to get that money too."

He dropped them off without turning around.

"All of y'all get out!"

When Toya said, "Bye, Young Ham."

He didn't respond.

$ $ $ $

Respect doesn't always feel good. Chase knew Young Ham was the realest one he'd ever seen. Not because of the cars or the money but because when it mattered, he showed up.

Still, there was truth underneath it all. Young Ham was his biggest influence. And that was dangerous. All that Chase did came from watching Young Ham do or say.

They walked in the house without speaking. Toya went straight to her room. Chase and L turned on the game and loaded up 2K. In the middle of a fast break where Chase was about to throw an alley-oop to Kobe, L paused it.

"Hold up."

He walked to the closet and came back holding the sack.

"Bro… some of the work missing. It's short."

Chase frowned. "Count it again."

"Nate, numbers is what I do. Missing is what I don't." L's voice was steady.

Chase's stomach dropped.

"How many?"

"Five."

The bag wasn't tied the way they left it.

"I believe you," Chase said quietly. "Something ain't right."

And just like that - the birthday glow dimmed.

LACE ME UP

Them lil' niggas done lost they mind. How you trade a personalized jersey for a hoodie and white tee? The game ain't that good. Then again... who am I to blame but myself?

Young Ham sat back on the leather sofa, staring at the ceiling. The house felt different now. Quieter. Rearranged into something that looked more like a bachelor's pad than a home. Since his shorty left, everything echoed.

He replayed the conversation with Chase and L over and over in his head. He hadn't led by example in any way. Hadn't practiced what he preached. He told them to chase scholarships while he chased plugs. Wanted them to stay clean while he dirtied his own hands.

What did he expect?

The streets had swallowed him whole once already, and spit him back out just polished enough to look like success. It was a vicious cycle dressed up as hustle.

He didn't want to watch his young homies fall victim to the same trap. But the hood bred that kind of ambition daily. And to make matters worse, he hadn't heard from Pop in months.

Pop had recently been transferred from Kansas to the federal facility in Beaumont - bloody Beaumont. Since then, no letters. No visits.

That didn't sit right.

$ $ $ $ $

Texas weather flipped more than gymnastics. It was forty degrees and biting cold.

Young Ham dressed proper for the road and told nobody where he was headed. He set the alarm, pulled out in a rented Yukon Denali, and hit the highway toward the BMT - Big Money Texas - the Golden Triangle.

After a thirty minute wait in a holding area, his name echoed over the intercom. He sat at the metal table first. Pop came out moments later, bigger than before, muscle stacked on muscle. Prison had hardened him, but it hadn't dulled his presence.

"Son, what brings you up here?" Pop grinned, wrapping him in a bear hug that stole the air from his lungs.

"Real talk, Pop. You don't look a day older than when they cuffed you. But I had to clear my head. Figured I'd dump it on your doorstep."

They laughed and sat down.

"Alright then. Since you here, give it to me straight."

Young Ham hesitated, but decided to rewind to the shootout.

"After I found out Killa did some foul shit. We had a face off that ended in gun smoke…he didn't make it." Young Ham paused and showed Pop his bullet wound. "They tried to hit me with a murder one, but a hundred-fifty thousand made it disappear."

Pop's jaw tightened. He knew about his nephew Base's death, but didn't know the rest. Pop rested both arms on the table top, letting his mind slip through the prison bars and razor wires…if only for a moment.

Young Ham leaned in and continued, breaking down how Ormiga and his henchmen executed Franco in front of him.

"Hold on," Pop interrupted. "You mean to tell me you met Ormiga?"

"Not just met him. I've been doing business with him since he offed Franco."

Pop leaned back, shaking his head slowly.

"Listen to me, son. Whatever Ormiga told you about Franco is a lie. He's been trying to take his position, claiming Franco had been blindsided by the so-called American dream, while his own country suffered."

"Ormiga said Franco was taking from the family, and that's why they took him out."

Pop chuckled.

"Taking what? Money? Franco could wipe his ass with hundred-dollar bills. That family been controlling ninety percent of the coke touching U.S. soil before it ever hit the streets."

"Another thing that tripped me out was Ormiga sported the exact ring you left in the lamp."

"That ring represents the cocaine king. The only way he possesses that is if Domingo Emilio Ochoa, aka Domino, has passed."

He went on, breaking it down.

"When the Villavicencio Cartel murdered Carlos, Franco's grandfather. A string of violent deaths left the cartel leader's head floating in the Buenaventura port. Domingo earned the nickname Domino because his adversaries fell one by one."

Young Ham rubbed his temples.

"So what that got to do with me?"

"Stop jumping the gun and listen," Pop said calmly. "Domino needed a Colombian body to run U.S. distribution. Franco and PePe were already stationed in America. That made Ormiga furious. He felt entitled but Domino knew his grandson was a hot head who'd have them warring with other drug lords."

Young Ham connected the dots.

"So I'm caught in the middle of a family feud."

"Exactly."

Pop lowered his voice.

"If Ormiga wanted you gone, you'd be gone. If Ormiga wanted you alive, he wouldn't have tried to flex in front of you. Somebody playing chess. You just on the board."

Silence sat between them.

"Now hear me clear," Pop added. "That lighter you saw with the Magnate-Rey symbol? That ain't just jewelry. That's legacy. Franco pictured this day coming and gave it to me. Told me use it wisely and don't fall victim to its power. Ormiga ain't right…I feel it. But stay where you at for now and I'll let you know something soon."

Young Ham nodded slowly.

Visiting hours had come to an end. He stood and embraced Pop, not knowing the next time they'd see each other again.

$ $ $ $ $

Nightfall.

Young Ham pulled into his condo driveway, engine still running. Franco had kept it real after all, and in return his people had played him. Pop's advice echoed in his head.

Stay where you at. Act like you know nothing.

Wait.

He considered going inside the empty house. But being alone didn't sound appealing. He reversed and headed somewhere he knew he'd be welcomed.

He knocked, even though he had a key. Adiva opened the door dressed to kill - sheer lingerie clinging to her curves, hair pressed down her back.

"Hey, king," she purred, stepping aside just enough for their bodies to brush.

"Where's Kenya and Queen?" he asked, settling onto the futon.

"Queen asleep. Kenya out with her girl."

Adiva walked over and straddled him slowly.

"I felt you coming before you got here," she whispered. "You taught me to listen to my body. It don't lie."

She slipped the teddy over her head, letting it fall.

"Now that you here… I hope you can hear it calling for you."

Young Ham stared - temptation heavy in the room. But his mind wasn't fully present. Because somewhere between cartel politics, and Monique's absence…something felt off.

TOUGH LOVE

Big Zeke sent Young Ham a clip of Youngin' doing a hundred down Airport Blvd on a Ninja bike, one-time right behind him with lights flashing.

Ever since Stacks caught fed time, Youngin' had been moving reckless - like he was trying to outrun something inside himself. Nothing anybody said stuck.

"Zeke, I can't keep overlookin' the fact he puttin' us all in jeopardy," Young Ham said, drained. "It ain't just the bike. It's the random beefing and the loud moves. I ride for mine whether they right or wrong… but the laws don't care about loyalty."

Big Zeke sighed. "I tried talking to him after he shot up that car at the carwash just 'cause dude was bumpin' that The Heights trapped harder than the Bricks. That nigga know damn well them boys in the rearview."

Young Ham leaned back, weighing it.

"What you think we oughta do, big homie?"

"You do what's best for the people who expect the best out you."

That was it.

Smiley would be back in town tomorrow. Young Ham wanted every member present when he addressed Youngin'.

$ $ $ $ $

"What y'all sayin'? I ain't hood no more?" Youngin' barked when they confronted him.

"You got outta control," Young Ham said evenly.

"Nigga, I rep this harder than anybody," Youngin' snapped. "And I'll bag anybody that disrespect CKC. So what if I have fun? I'm young. We young. Ain't nobody tryna live like yo Pops."

Nobody spoke.

The silence said enough.

Youngin' looked around and saw it - they were done babysitting him. No matter how many kilos he pushed, it wasn't worth the headache.

"You know what? Fuck all y'all," he spat, throwing up the middle finger. "I'll put the hood on my back myself."

"Slow down, kinfolk," Big Zeke warned.

"I ain't slowing shit." Youngin' laughed bitter. "Nigga, you was broke before I put you on. You got the nerve to side with this nigga."

Smiley stepped in. "We family, man. Where the love at?"

Youngin' turned on him. "Love? Where was the love when Killa got smoked, huh?"

There it was.

The grudge he'd been holding finally surfaced. Young Ham felt it hit his chest, but he stayed seated.

"Homie, this ain't for us, so I'm not goin' there with you," he said calmly.

Youngin' stepped closer.

"That King of the Bricks title? That don't mean nothing. You just living off yo Pop's name."

He crossed a line.

Young Ham rose slowly.

"Is you smokin' dope or dog food? Ain't a time or place I ain't stood tall on my own two. From the trap to the jailhouse. Don't play with me."

They squared up.

Youngin' swung first - wild.

The punch grazed off, but the next one connected, snapping Young Ham's head back. He answered with a sharp combination.

Big Zeke grabbed Youngin' from behind before it escalated further.

"Chill out, fam. Leave it alone." Big Zeke held tight until Youngin' calmed down.

"If that's how it is," Youngin' yelled, wiping blood from his lip, "then I'm out."

He walked to the door, paused, and looked back. "From the birth to the dirt. Remember that."

The door slammed.

Silence again.

They all knew what it meant. Youngin' had been there since day one. Now somebody had to fill that production gap. One hundred bricks every thirty days didn't replace itself.

Smiley tried to lighten it. "Give it time. We'll piece it together."

But time wasn't working on their side. The next drop was days away. It was expected to be bigger than the original shipment.

Then Young Ham's social line buzzed.

"Young Ham, please come get me," she said, breath shaky. "This lady crazy. She my mama but I'ma beat her ass if she put her hands on me."

"What happened?"

"All I know is she barged in my room arguing at me for nothing. I think she high."

"Where Nate and Larry?"

"I called them first. They said they're on their way."

"Stay calm. I'm coming."

Ten minutes later, Young Ham pulled up to Jewel's house. The yelling could be heard from outside. The door burst open. Toya stood there with a backpack slung over her shoulder.

"Leave, bitch!" Jewel screamed from inside. "Don't come back. I should've let them white folks keep your hot ass."

Young Ham stepped inside.

Jewel rocked back and forth on the couch, an unlit cigarette hung loosely between her bony fingers. Her pupils were blown wide. Her lips were cracked, and dried blood caked at the corners.

"Jewel, what's wrong?" he asked carefully.

"Don't come in here like you the preacher's son," she snapped. "You fucking my daughter and got my son working for you. I oughta call the laws on your nasty ass."

Young Ham saw it clearly now.

Relapse.

Chase and L rushed in.

"Mama, what you doing?"

"Don't mama me," she screamed. "You brought that poison back in my house. It's that no good bastards fault. That nigga right there got me strung out in the first place."

Every head turned toward Dopefiend J standing in the doorway.

He didn't deny it.

"She telling the truth about me," he said quietly. "I introduced her to the game. That's something I regret every day."

"Wait." Chase said, confused. "You and my mama know each other?"

"Huh, know each other." Jewel said. "Boy, that's your coward ass daddy."

"Mama, what you mean he my daddy?"

"Like I said. He your damn daddy. But I'm telling you now he ain't about a damn thang."

"Look, son. I mean, Chase." Dopefiend J said. "Its a long story but we can sit down whenever you ready."

"He ready now!" Jewel hollered. "Because all of y'all can hit the door."

Toya grabbed Young Ham's arm.

"Can we go?"

He nodded.

Toya slung her backpack inside the truck, then climbed in. Young Ham crunk up and waited on the boys. His doors were always open to either of them.

Chase and L came out carrying stuffed bedsheets over their shoulders. They headed his way.

"Young Ham, I need to holler at my old man." Chase said after him and L chunked their bedrolls over the truck bed.

"Go handle yo business, lil gee. Y'all know where I'm at."

Young Ham gave them a pound, sending them on their way. He thought back to a night when he was fresh off the porch, soaking up free game from Pop….

Late one night, Young Ham accidently barged in on Pop wiping down bullets with a turtle green face towel. Pop looked up before feeding another brass slug into the clip. Chink.

"What I tell you about protecting the money." Pop said, voice echoing.

Young Ham stepped further inside the room, smiling slightly. He knew Pop was doing a game check-up, his favorite time.

"You said if you can't afford losing it, don't front it."

"What I say about someone playing with yo money."

"You said if a nigga owe you, go take it. And if you feel like a nigga owe you, go take it."

Pop nodded.

"What's rule number one?"

"Its all about that money!" Young Ham said, on a roll.

"What's rule number two, then?" Pop pressured.

He had forgotten.

"I don't know what's rule number two, Pop. I forgot."

Pop paused.

"Nah, son. You ain't forget rule number two because there is no rule number two. If it ain't about the money… it ain't about nothing."

Young Ham had remembered that night like it was yesterday, and had always kept it about that money.

His young homie was now falling in line where he had begun. Before he let him be watered down, getting the game elsewhere. He'll give it like it was given, and lace him up about rule number one: It's all about that money!

LIFE IS CRAZY

"This shit unbelievable," Chase muttered, staring out the windshield.

He never imagined one day he'd be riding in a car with his father - a man absent his whole life - and that the first time they locked eyes would be over a drug transaction.

He glanced at Dopefiend J behind the wheel and shook his head.

"Chase, I know you probably wondering where I been your whole life," Dopefiend J said calmly.

"Man, you reading my mind or what?" Chase snapped. "I'm sixteen, and our first encounter is you buying a piece of dope from me. Life too crazy right now."

Dopefiend J exhaled slowly.

"I told you I'd break it down when you was ready to cross that bridge. Guess we here."

He paused.

The year was 1994. I was on top of the world.

Back then I ran with a crew called BTC - Booker T Circle. That was before the youngsters started screaming this new wave stuff about the Bricks. We had money, cars, respect. Every weekend the block parties popped outside Casanova. Ballers, players, hustlers, and even gangsters- all of us shoulder to shoulder like kings.

Police stayed away. Figured we'd destroy each other eventually.

I pushed a '84 Seville, metallic gold, chrome and gold disks through the city like I owned the town. Kept a briefcase full of hundreds in the trunk. If I felt like making it rain, I made it flood.

I was clocking millions and felt untouchable. Until I snorted my first line. I watched my homies toot and still move sharp, so I convinced myself it wouldn't slow me down. They sold it to me like it was fuel. Like it made you better and kept your dick hard for all the ladies dropping panties left and right.

It didn't.

It owned me.

My hustle slipped. My judgment blurred. I stayed dressed and acted like I had control, but I was drowning quietly. Then one night at Club Phases, I crossed a line I couldn't uncross.

This freak pulled out crack rocks and sprinkled them over the weed. She had my dick and balls in her mouth saying I'd feel like I was getting a blow job on the moon. I told myself, You only live once.

That lie cost me everything.

Over time I burned every bridge I had. Nobody trusted me. I started snatching purses to survive. Jewel tried to love me through it. She was pregnant with you and still believed I'd get clean.

I didn't.

I spiraled.

After ducking debts and dodging faces, I went to J-Rich , an old school hustler with real weight.

"Give a playa some dap for old times sake," I told him.

"If it ain't my man, Money Black."

Money Black was my name when chasing paper was my game. Now that the paper was gone, I was left just being black as a mutherfucker.

"Check me out, cool breeze," I told him. "I'm trying to get off my knees and back on my feet. Front me one so I can make two. Then come back and spend it with you."

He looked at me like I was already dead.

"Money Black, I'ma make that happen. It's blood on my money so live and die on yo word."

"Don't worry, boss man. On my grandma I got you."

J-Rich fronted me.

I smoked it.

Every last gram.

Now I owed money I couldn't repay.

I got word J-Rich and his boys were looking for me. So I told your mama we was leaving town. If she wanted to come, she had till morning.

She didn't show.

I sold a pair of Gators for a bus ticket, hopped on a Greyhound, and ran as far as my pockets would take me. Texarkana, Tx. Where not a soul knew me or what I was running from.

"That was sixteen years ago and I'm just coming back. I figured J-Rich was either dead or locked up. He was both. He caught a fed case and came home too fast. The same young boys that rode for him ended up riding down on him."

Chase sat quiet for a moment.

"When I ran across an old smoking buddy. He hipped me that your mama and a white girl I got pregnant before leaving, both had boys around the same age."

Dopefiend J pulled up in the Bricks.

"I even promised God that if he bought my two boys in my life, then I'd stop smoking."

Chase laughed dry.

"You knew it was me when we first met. Why you ain't say nothing?"

"'Cause I saw myself in you," Dopefiend J said. "And I didn't know what to say to my prayer getting heard, let alone getting answered."

"Guess you lied to God," L said, laughing, "'cause you still smoking."

Dopefiend J rolled the window down.

"No I didn't and no I ain't. I didn't get both boys but I'll take what he gave me. I ain't here to be your father. I forfeited that. What I can do is help y'all swell y'all pockets the right way. I done seen the game from both sides."

He flicked his lighter and straight shooter out on the street.

"It's on y'all now."

FOLLOW-UP

Monique sat in her car for a full three minutes before getting out. The building didn't look like a place where lives changed. Just another downtown office with tinted windows and clean bricks.

She hated that. Because nothing about what she was about to do felt ordinary.

She stepped inside. The air smelled like copy machine paper and burnt coffee. The receptionist didn't look up long enough to care who she was.

"Second floor. Last door on the left," the woman said.

Monique's heels echoed down the hallway like they were announcing her.

Agent Woods stood when she entered.

She didn't smile.

"You came."

"I said I would."

She gestured toward the chair across from her. "You understand this doesn't work halfway, Monique."

Her jaw flexed.

"I'm not here to debate. I'm here to listen."

Natasha folded her hands.

"That's a start."

She slid a thin folder across the desk. Inside were photos. Young Ham outside a warehouse. Big Zeke stepping off a plane in Nevada. Smiley at a dock in Louisiana.

Monique's breath stalled.

"You've been watching them."

"For years." Natasha confirmed.

"You could've arrested him."

"We don't want him arrested," Natasha said evenly. "We want him dismantled."

The word hit her differently.

Dismantled.

Like something built wrong.

Monique stared at the pictures. She remembered hospital rooms. Bandages. Court dates. The way he held her when she cried. The way he lied just as easy.

"What exactly are you asking me to do?" she asked quietly.

"We're asking you to tell us when something changes. Any sudden moves. You don't have to create anything. Just confirm what we already suspect."

"And if I don't?"

Natasha didn't blink.

"Then when we move on without you."

Silence stretched between them.

"You're not trying to save him," she said. "You're trying to bury him."

"We're trying to end it."

Monique leaned back in her chair and stared at the ceiling. "If I say yes," she asked, "you protect me?"

"Yes."

"And him?"

Natasha paused.

"We protect cooperation."

That wasn't the answer she wanted.

Monique closed the folder.

"I'm not promising you loyalty," she said carefully. "I'm promising you awareness."

Natasha nodded once.

"That's enough for now."

She stood.
Then she walked out.

Hard But Its Fair

Federal judge Philip Ross, Assistant District Attorney Bran Myers, and Randy Cummings sat inside a summer retreat overlooking Lake Austin.

"Welcome, Ms. Natasha," Cummings said, closing the door behind him. "Glad you could join us."

"Thank you, Randy," Natasha smirked. "But it's my pleasure accompanying you fellows today."

"Perfect. Then have a seat and let's get started shall we. Before your arrival I spoke with Philip and Bran about my position once I retire. I recommended to them your credentials."

"Oh stop, Randy. You're making me blush." Natasha fanned. "As you all know, I will bring every case and individual that crosses my desk to justice," she finished smoothly.

"Excellent," Randy said, loosening his tie. "Now let's loosen up a bit."

Natasha crossed her legs and leaned back. "What do you have in mind?"

"Humph, now that you ask. Me and the boys would like to have ourselves a good time. If that's alright with you, my dear."

"Not a problem. I've always been a team player."

$ $ $ $ $

"Man, you gotta be kidding me," Dopefiend J said, shaking his head. "Ko-Baby is yo old man."

Young Ham, Chase, L, and Dopefiend J sat in the condo living room catching up on history in real time.

"That's why you look so familiar," Dopefiend J continued. "Your old man and uncles were solid. Back when we was having money, so was they. My partner Joe started messing with your mama. I warned him."

Toya entered with drinks. Dopefiend J's eyes lingered a second too long when she handed him a root beer.

"I told Joe he was playing with fire in somebody else's backyard," Dopefiend J said. "He ain't listen. Got his head split for it. You're too young to remember that though."

"Nah, I'm with you," Young Ham said. "But what's with you and my lil' homie? Too late to play daddy don't you think."

Dopefiend J nodded slowly. "You right. I ain't trying to replace nothing. I made a promise though. If I ever got the chance to meet my sons, I'd get clean. I'm ready to help him any way I can."

Young Ham studied him.

"For some reason, I believe you. But this what we gon' do 'cause I don't move off emotion. You got three weeks. They say habits break in twenty-one days. So as of right now… you on the clock."

"I like that," Dopefiend J replied. "Three weeks gon' feel like a lifetime trying to tie down this addiction, but I don't got nobody and nowhere to go."

"Ima help you but you gotta help yoself first," Young Ham continued. " You gon' sleep in the garage. I'll put a couch and a fridge of food so you don't leave unless it's necessary. In return, you keep my yard cut, cars clean, and your system clean."

"One more thing," Dopefiend J grinned. "I don't care about no food but I'ma need candy and cigarettes 'cause I'ma be jonesing harder than a mutha."

Three weeks later, the man who walked out the garage wasn't Dopefiend J anymore. He had gained a quick ten pounds, and filled out in the shoulders from concrete pushups. Eyes clearer. He smoked Newports and chewed gummy worms like a kid, but the crackhead glaze was gone.

"Call me Black Jesus," he said. "If God pulled me out that pit, and Jesus dirtied his sandals messing around the hood and heard my prayers. He gotta be Black."

Black Jesus smirked. "What you say, Young Ham. Work me in slow."

"I'ma link you with yo son and his partner as they doorman," Young Ham decided. "Sharpen they game while building that relationship."

Chase and L had taken over Youngin's old apartment in the Bricks and were moving weight like disciplined young wolves. No more Lil Nate and Lil Larry energy. They were serious now.

Black Jesus gave them old-school lessons with new-school twists - how to cook it right, cut it smart, weigh it exact, and break it down clean.

Meanwhile, Young Ham expanded. He pulled into Kingston Village and watched the hand-to-hand traffic from behind tint. It was booming. Block-bleeding youngsters moved careless with no structure, chasing cars in broad daylight.

"These kids making all this money with no guidance," he thought.

After hitting the Marshalls and Elmeridge, he knew the pattern.

Tap. Tap. Tap.

Two block-bleeders from the Courts knocked on his tinted window.

"What's up?" Young Ham said calmly. "Can I help y'all?"

"Nah, but we can help you find your way off the block if you lost?" one said.

"This Muncy block and he don't take it kindly on niggas short stopping." the other one jumped in.

"Muncy Harris off Paquita?" Young Ham asked.

Both of them froze.

"Yeah, nigga."

"Call him," Young Ham said. "Tell him Young Ham from the Bricks outside."

The attitude shifted instantly.

"The King of the Bricks? Why you ain't say that?"

He was escorted upstairs to the Courts' headquarters. Muncy welcomed him with a fist lock and chest bump.

"I know damn well you ain't here unless it's about money."

"No doubt," Young Ham replied. "You running it solid. But we both know the plug matter more than pride. On behalf of the Cash Keepers, I'm offering better numbers, better product, and a guaranteed boost in profit."

Muncy hesitated. His current connect was inconsistent but familiar. "Let me chew on it."

Young Ham left with a calm confidence that three out of four territories were leaning his way. Kingston Village. The Marshalls. Elmeridge.

The kingdom was widening.

A Reason for Everything

Ever since Monique made the decision to surveil Young Ham, luck had shifted. For weeks, she felt like she was chasing smoke - nothing concrete enough to file, nothing airtight enough to submit. Young Ham moved carefully, methodical in his dealings. Even when he pumped gas, he angled his face just enough to avoid a full capture.

He was disciplined.

But lately something had changed.

That sixth sense that once kept him five steps ahead of everyone else seemed dulled. And while that wasn't like him, Monique wasn't complaining. Her black evidence folder was growing thick.

What she still needed was one clean photograph tying him directly to his unknown supplier - the man responsible for funneling serious weight into the Cash Keepers' operation. She already had photos of product in Young Ham's possession, but what she lacked was the bridge.

"Good evening, Ms. Thorton," Natasha said smoothly. "What can I do for you?"

"I'm doing well, Agent Woods," Monique replied.

"I wanted to inform you that I'll be concluding my investigation shortly. I would, however, like to request a brief extension in order to submit something thorough and substantial."

Natasha's smile faded the moment the line went silent. The nerve. Who does she think she is, asking for an extension like we're working on her clock?

She masked her irritation instantly.

"You must really be onto something," Natasha said sweetly. "I look forward to reviewing your findings. Let's say… one week from today."

Monique knew exactly what that tone meant. Natasha wanted her to rush. Wanted her to fail. She hung up and sat on the edge of her hotel bed replaying the conversation. She said she couldn't wait to review my findings. That makes two of us.

$ $ $ $ $

After laying the groundwork and renting upstairs apartments inside Kingston Village, The Marshalls, and Elmeridge. Young Ham was ready to press the gas. He and Big Zeke sat in the Navigator breaking it down.

"So we just pull up and open shop?" Big Zeke asked, "and expect to be welcomed?"

"I scoped it," Young Ham replied calmly. "They don't got no major work over there. When dealers run low, they gotta call across town. That's weak."

Big Zeke nodded. "So we put supply right in they face."

"Exactly. We play it cool at first. Then we tighten up on anybody not buying from us."

"How many heads we need?"

"Three. One for each complex."

"I thought you was eyeing the Courts too."

Young Ham shook his head. "Muncy run that. I ain't trying to strong-arm somebody I respect. But eventually? Everybody gonna have to choose."

"I can dig it." Big Zeke liked the sound of that. "Are we pulling three top earners off the block? It'll be sort of a grinder's promotion."

"You got someone in mind?"

"Damn, right." Big Zeke grinned. "Two hardheads and a female grimier than them put together."

"Let's do it."

$$\$\ \$\ \$\ \$\ \$$$

Kenya had just returned from upstate New York after attending her grandmother's funeral. She came back disciplined and focused.

Not only was she ready to establish another route out of state, she also brought something valuable with her. Her Islamic-faith older brother, Jalil. A money-washing specialist with international connections and a network that stretched beyond state lines.

Young Ham flew to New York to meet him personally. If Jalil was going to touch Cash Keepers' money, he needed to look him in the eye.

"Your name carries weight with my sister," Jalil said inside his Mount Pleasant estate, his home away from home. "That's rare. I normally don't socialize where I sleep. But I wanted you to know I live to do this, and do this to live."

A scanty dressed waitress entered with colorful drinks on a silver platter. When Young Ham did drink, he preferred straight no chaser. But being a guest today, he sipped lightly.

"Young Ham, two percent off every million-dollar transaction," Jalil said. "Your money becomes invisible."

Young Ham calculated quickly and agreed to give Jalil a go. On the flight home, he arranged for Kenya and Queen to drive separate vehicles back to New York with $500,000 hidden in each trunk.

$$\$\ \$\ \$\ \$\ \$$$

The plane landed at Bergstrom around six. Young Ham barely cleared the terminal before his phone rang.

"Young Ham!" Casandra cried. "They shot him."

Everything inside him locked up.

"Calm down," he said, moving faster toward his truck. "Tell me what happened."

"He was in Craigwood buying smoke from Tank. He started arguing with some LHC dudes in the street. They started fighting.

Then one of the Cavanaugh brothers ran up and shot him twice."

Young Ham's jaw tightened.

Why this nigga gotta be so hard-headed?

"Where you at?" he asked.

"St. David's," she sobbed. "The doctors said he lost too much blood… he might not make it."

Young Ham's expansion plans, money laundering routes, territory grabs - none of that mattered in that moment. If Youngin didn't pull through, the streets weren't just going to get messy. They were going to get personal.

Staying On Point

An H2 hearse led the motorcade like a general marching a fallen soldier to his last command. Four black Hummers followed close behind, carrying grief behind tinted glass. The city moved around them unaware, but inside that procession, everything felt suspended.

Youngin's mother, Ms. Joyce, rode alone. No conversation. No music. Just the weight of a son she'd never see again.

Behind her was Casandra and her family, trying to be strong for one another. And behind them rolled the Cash Keepers - Big Zeke, Smiley, Young Ham, Chase, L, Black Jesus - dressed in black suits and matching hats embroidered with bold white CKC letters that seemed larger than life.

The Nigerian trio and Toya trailed the line, closing it out like soldiers finishing formation.

The cemetery filled fast with family, friends, and close associates. Reverend E.M. Jolly spoke about purpose and seasons, about lives that burn bright but not long. But when the casket lowered into the earth, no words mattered.

One by one, the Cash Keepers stepped forward and placed their hats on top of the rose-and-gold casket.

A final salute.

Tears rolled down Big Zeke's face openly. Smiley didn't bother wiping his. Young Ham stood longer than the rest, staring down into the grave like he was trying to memorize it.

"You ain't a stranger," Young Ham told Casandra after hugging her tight and kissing Ms. Joyce's cheek. "You family now. Anything you or that lil' one need call me."

When it was done, he walked away alone for a moment. Not to mourn but to think. Because grief and business never stayed separate for long.

Three days passed.
Young Ham barely slept and ate even less. The house felt quiet in ways he didn't like. He was barely bouncing back from Youngin's absence. But today wasn't about loss. It was about Ormiga.

The foreign plug had made it clear he wanted a proper introduction to "real soul food" during his visit to the capital city. Young Ham chose Mama Diva's, one of the clean fronts he'd built with Jalil's help.

Technically, enchiladas belonged to Mexico, but the way Mrs. Pam and her identical twin layered them with seasoning and pride, they tasted like southern hospitality wrapped in tortillas. After his first bite months ago, Young Ham had given them raises on the spot.

"These almost taste like my momma's," he'd told them.

They smiled like that meant everything.

Because it did.

$ $ $ $ $

Across town, Monique woke before her alarm.
Energy surged through her like electricity. This was the moment she'd built toward for weeks. Forty days of surveillance, piecing patterns together like a puzzle no one else could solve.

Private investigator Monique Thorton was about to capture the final image that federal agents couldn't.

A fresh tracker vehicle had been cleared for today. She parked early at Mama Diva's and blended into the lunchtime crowd, settling into a position in the lot with a clean line of sight through the restaurant's glass windows.

There he was.

Young Ham.

And across from him sat a Latino man she'd only heard referenced in whispers. She was confident the well dressed gentleman was the King of the Bricks' infamous cocaine supplier.

Her heart kicked harder.

Inside, Young Ham and Ormiga sat in a booth against the glass. Usually, Ormiga traveled with armed security pressed tight to his sides. Today, they stood outside near the entrance.

"Young Ham," Ormiga began. "Where I come from, men your age are only allowed to pull triggers. You impress me."

"All that's fine," Young Ham replied evenly. "But I need to be notified upfront if the business structure changes."

Ormiga's eyes flickered for a half-second. "Point taken," he said. Then leaned in. "What I say now does not leave this table."

Young Ham nodded once, a gesture that would've had Pop jumping from his seat right now. Thinking about it made Young Ham smirk.

"The extra cocaine you received," Ormiga said, lowering his voice, "is what I call ghost coke. Let me explain. I'm in charge of U.S shipping. If I say three hundred, five hundred kilos has been seized. I go unquestioned. Do you see where I'm going?"

Young Ham didn't blink. Ormiga was skimming.

Not just skimming - stealing under the cover of authority.

Pop's words echoed in the back of his mind: A thief is worse than a liar. A liar tells you what you want to hear. A thief tells you nothing.

"So what's your endgame?" Young Ham asked calmly.

Ormiga lifted his hand and tapped the Magnate-Rey ring he wore proudly.

"This here represents power and respect. I will stop at nothing until I'm respected and feared throughout Colombia."

A teenaged waitress brought their plates and drinks to the table. They thanked her and agreed to give her a shout if they needed anything else.

Young Ham gazed out the window and kept one eye sweeping over the cars in the parking lot as Ormiga went on.

"Oh, shit! Did he see me?" Monique wondered as she slid lower into her seat.

She had zoned out and tried to snap a perfect facial shot of the Latino kingpin when, all of a sudden, Young Ham looked straight out the window. The look wasn't random either. It felt like it cut directly through the glass.

For a moment she froze, forcing herself to breathe slow and steady so the lump in her throat could settle. Once the panic passed, the courage came creeping back.

Monique peeked over the dashboard. Young Ham had already gone back to eating again.

Whew! That was close, she thought. I'm going to stay low and get what I came for without blowing my cover. What the fuck!

Young Ham kept his attention on Ormiga while casually lifting his fork. To anyone else sitting in that restaurant, he looked like a man simply finishing his dinner. But Monique noticed something strange.

Each time he raised the fork, the movement lingered just a second too long. At first she brushed it off. Then it happened again.

Young Ham twirled the fork slowly between his fingers before bringing it toward his mouth. The motion looked natural, almost lazy, but there was a rhythm to it now. A pattern.

Monique leaned slightly forward in her seat, eyes narrowing as she watched through the camera lens.

No way.

Young Ham cut his eyes toward the window again without turning his head. Just a quick glance - the kind of look a man gives when he already knows what's out there. Then he did it again. Sign language.

Fork up.

Pause.

Two small taps against the plate.

Fork down.

Monique felt the hairs on the back of her neck stand up. Her breath caught in her chest as the realization hit her. He's talking to me. She recalled how the two of them sat in the wee hours, practicing a skill learned from her real estate days of coming in contact with deaf clients.

Young Ham kept his expression calm, nodding along to whatever Ormiga was saying, but the fork kept moving. Another small tap.

Monique sat frozen behind the dashboard, heart thumping against her ribs. Through the glass she could see him now - not just eating, but performing.

Across the parking lot, Monique swallowed hard.

Because now she understood something she hadn't expected to learn today. Young Ham hadn't just noticed her. He'd noticed her a long time ago.

And instead of exposing her….He was letting her sit there and wonder why.

Without warning, tears streamed down her face as she sat up straight and read aloud what he was telling her.

Forgive me. I'm sorry. Come back. And finally… I love you.

When he finished, she wiped her face dry, turned the ignition, and drove away.

Bingo.

Young Ham had almost missed her when she ducked down. Had it not been for that micro-second reflection off her camera, Monique probably would've slipped away unnoticed.

He had known from day one that the feds had put Monique on him.

Federal agent Randy Cummings had side-hustled and worked on Franco's payroll for years, long before the big man was falsely accused of stealing and then unjustly murdered by Ormiga.

Franco had paid handsomely to keep Young Ham and his crew under Randy Cummings' protection umbrella with the locals. Whenever key intelligence about the Cash Keepers' operations hit their "special bulletin," Randy Cummings quietly tipped Young Ham off.

"As I was mentioning," Ormiga said calmly, "to be respected and feared is what I seek most. When I killed Franco, it was because he had neither. I cannot allow that among my own people."

He paused, letting the words settle.

"He would have died sooner, but because of his rank and influence, I could not touch him without permission. I had to devise a treasonous infraction that would justify his execution. Now you understand when I say I stop at nothing to get what I want."

Right then and there, had Young Ham been carrying his strap, he would've emptied the entire clip into Ormiga's face-on behalf of Franco, a man who had kept it real in more ways than one.

Pop had been right when he first sensed something foul about Ormiga. The man carried himself like he invented the game, like he was slicker than baby oil and twice as dangerous. But Young Ham knew better. And now, he was seeing the full picture.

Ormiga made himself look like some type of don in America, as Franco actually was. But turns out Ormiga was who he said he was… a little ant. He would have to find out the hard way that the Black man invented the use of the word slick.

Young Ham pushed his plate to the center of the table. He had lost his appetite, unable to stomach any more of Ormiga's disgusting presence. Ormiga did the same, wiping his mouth as they both prepared to leave.

"Yo, what's next, chief?" Young Ham asked, already knowing the answer.

"You can expect to hear from me no later than two weeks," Ormiga said, standing. "We will go back to the original three hundred kilos. People have been poking their noses around, asking questions about shipments not arriving. I have to play it cool for now."

After a firm handshake, Ormiga excused himself and left. Young Ham remained seated, swirling the last of his drink while taking a moment to weigh the chance he had taken with Monique.

He let out a slow breath.

He finished his Hennessy in one slow swallow and pressed the stop button on his watch. Time always tells the truth. He peeled a hundred-dollar bill from his stack and left it on the table for Toya before walking out.

But the game was far from over.

The Net Tightens

Monique didn't drive straight back to the hotel.

She circled twice. Once to make sure she wasn't being followed. Twice to calm her breathing.

By the time she parked in the underground garage, her nerves had settled but her mind hadn't. She replayed the lunch meeting over and over. The way Young Ham scanned the parking lot like K9 instincts lived in his bloodstream.

Inside her suite, she uploaded the photos immediately. The image of Young Ham and Ormiga sharing that booth was clean enough to raise eyebrows in any federal courtroom. She attached the files and dialed.

"Agent Woods."

"Ms. Thorton," Natasha answered smoothly. "I was beginning to think you'd disappeared."

Monique ignored the tone.

"I have him," she said simply.

Silence.

"Explain."

"His high-level supplier is a foreign national.They met today. I have visuals."

Another pause.

"Come in tomorrow morning. Eight sharp."

The line went dead.

But across town, in a federal building with too many glass windows, Natasha Woods wasn't smiling. She was moving.

Within an hour, subpoenas were drafted. By nightfall, a joint task force call would be scheduled before sunrise.

Because what Monique didn't know-was that the feds were about to move Young Ham's name from "person of interest" to "priority target."

.

Down For The Crown

Monique drove to the federal building with a calm she did not entirely feel. The restaurant meeting had confirmed what her emotions had been whispering for weeks, and now there was no more middle ground to stand on.

She had made a choice, and whatever consequences followed would be hers to carry. By the time she stepped through the glass doors, her posture was straight and her expression unreadable, the look of a woman who understood that letting the cards fall where they may often costs something.

"Good to see you, Ms. Thorton," Natasha said, smiling the kind of smile that never reached her eyes. "I'm glad you could make it."

Monique studied her for a second.

"Ms. Woods, with all due respect, this has been the most twisted case I've ever taken on. It has tested me both personally and professionally. But I didn't cut corners."

Natasha barely blinked. Monique could have spared the boring speech, for all she cared.

"Well, let's see if it's worth anything."

"Oh, believe me," Monique said with a smile. "These pictures are priceless."

Monique slid a thick manila envelope across the desk. Natasha snatched it, flipped it open, and let the photos spill out across the surface. Natasha's composure cracked for half a second.

"What is this?"

"What it looks like, bitch." Monique said calmly. "You getting cum drunk off old white men's spoiled milk."

Natasha's eyes darted between the images, recalculating everything she thought she knew. Monique leaned forward with her phone and snapped a photo.

"You see, I'm in love with the man you want to put behind bars. For doing nothing other than surviving this white man's world. So back off, bitch."

Silence stretched. Monique turned and walked out before Natasha could regain control. But the story didn't end there.

The Parking Lot

Randy Cummings called before she made it home.

"Can we talk?"

They met in a Starbucks parking lot. He stayed behind the wheel when she pulled up beside him. Tinted windows. Engine idling.

She got in.

He didn't waste time.

"You did good," he said, handing her an envelope.

"Keep the check. And tell Young Ham I said hello."

That part made her stomach tighten. This wasn't about justice. This was positioning the power of control. And Natasha wasn't nearly as in control as she believed.

Natasha wore her hair straight and spoke like she belonged in rooms that locked others out. She thought a polished upbringing made her superior.

What she didn't understand was that Randy would never allow her to run the department, no matter how much he loved her sexual pleasures.

Monique saw through both of them now. The system wasn't clean. It was layered with filth. And everybody was playing angles. She drove from the parking lot in silence.

She'd never told anyone the full story about her father. When she was little, he was her hero. A street legend who spoiled his baby girl and called her princess. Until the day the feds kicked the door in.

Her heart was shattered because of a man who chose the streets over his family. She had built walls after that, promising herself she would never love another man who made his living in the fast lane.

But Young Ham wasn't her father.

He was disciplined. He didn't move recklessly. He was calculated. And that difference changed everything. She was choosing her man instead of a badge.

She still had the key to his condo.

Before she reached his place, she stopped at the post office. She mailed a letter and photos to her father in federal custody. No explanation. Just a quiet message that she understood now.

Sticking To The Plan

Though the stakes were rising, Young Ham tightened up and pieced everything together the way Pop had taught him. Trying to predict the full outcome of what happened at Mama Diva's was premature. Hope alone wasn't strategy. For him, that situation was just the beginning. Part two was already loading.

He left the house early that morning, trying to shake Monique off his mind as he rode through the Bricks to check on Chase and L at the bottom of the hill. The bass from his truck rolled down the block before he did.

"What it do, Young Ham?" L called out, stepping outside first. Chase and Black Jesus followed behind him.

"You got it, hustler," Young Ham replied, standing in the truck door. "I just came by to holler at y'all before I park it for the day. It always feel good coming back to where it started."

"Amen to that!" Chase said, as he and Young Ham hit their signature handshake. Even Black Jesus had caught on by now, completing the pound without missing a beat.

"On some real, Young Ham," Chase asked, getting straight to business, "how many ounces you can pull out of a brick if we dropping them at twenty grams a piece?"

"Chase, I already told you," Black Jesus cut in. "You can bring back fifty if you cooking it right."

"Yeah, I know," Chase shrugged, "but I wanted to hear what Young Ham was gon' say."

Young Ham peeped the look on Black Jesus' face before the man turned and went back inside. Chase and L had grown into full-fledged trappers. There was no such thing as part-time hustling to them. Taking days off was for people who didn't understand what they were building.

"Look," Young Ham said calmly, "don't rush the math. If you know the science, you already know the answer. Just make sure y'all thinking long-term, not quick flips."

"Say less," L nodded.

"Let me back up outta here and let y'all get it on," Young Ham added, giving the young go-getters a pound. "Be easy and keep it hustling."

"At all times!" Chase announced, patting his noticeably fat pockets.

Young Ham shook his head. "Don't be a show-off, lil' homie. True ballers don't pat their pockets."

They laughed, but they heard him.

Before heading back to the crib, Young Ham cruised through the East and hopped out on a couple of the blocks he supplied. Even though he was major paid and lived comfortably out with the white folks now, showing his face in the hood was mandatory. Respect had to be maintained in person.

"What's jumpin', Speedy? Y'all good?" Young Ham called out as he stepped across the street.

"Shit gravy, my G," Speedy replied, flashing his grill. "That bag comin' your way in a day or two. We almost flat on that last issue you sent."

"Just holler when y'all ready and it's on," Young Ham assured him.

He didn't stick around long. You never knew who was watching, and lingering too comfortably was careless.

Fifteen minutes and four songs later, Young Ham pulled up to the condo. The place was quiet. He kicked off his shoes and moved toward the bedroom, only to stop when two bully puppies raced towards him. The dogs were leashed by a banner that read:

I-Love-U.

Monique stood there holding a black folder tight against her chest. Tears slid down her face.

"Please forgive me, Foreal," she said softly. "For not being at your side like a hustler's wife supposed to be. I understand now that street men need love too. I'm ready to be yours whether you winning big or sitting in a jail cell."

Young Ham stepped forward and silenced her with a deep, deliberate kiss. When he pulled back, he took the folder from her hands and flipped through the pictures inside. He led her over to the sofa and confessed his rocks to riches story.

Monique kissed him softly. "It don't matter, baby. I ain't going nowhere. Enough of that though. I need me some of that thug love."

They tore each other's clothes off in seconds, going at it hard like it was the first time. Then went upstairs and grinded their bodies under the streams of a hot shower.

"So tell me," she asked later, her head resting across his chest, "how you knew I was following you?"

"I been doing this, babygirl," he replied smoothly.

"I read signs. I listen to the body. And it never hurt having people in high places… you feel me?"

She knew exactly who he was referring to.

"And since you were gone," he continued, "Chase, his daddy, L, and Toya moved in. Long story. I'll fill you in later. But I think we need our own place."

He sat up, serious now.

"Tomorrow I gotta leave town. I'll be back in three days. It's important. I gotta iron some things out before I move forward. While I'm gone, I want you staying at a hotel while looking for a house. If you see it and want it… buy it."

$ $ $ $ $

Phoenix, Arizona

It was ten o'clock West Coast time when Young Ham landed in Phoenix. The flight gave him space to digest part two of Pop's grand scheme. If everything aligned the way it was supposed to, this trip would open doors that stretched beyond the hood.

He checked his watch, irritated that his ride hadn't pulled up yet.

"Where this fool at?" he muttered. "Got me standing out here like a lost tourist."

An all-black Audi A8 eased to a stop in front of him, its tinted windows impossible to see through. The back passenger window lowered halfway.

"Young Ham, get in," a voice said.

He opened the door without hesitation.

"Nice to meet you, Young Ham. Me name is Juanito, but Juan is fine. Sit back and relax. We will discuss more once we get to me home."

The man beside him stared straight ahead like a trained killer. Young Ham studied him the same way.

They drove nearly an hour before arriving at a custom-built estate tucked behind private gates in Casa Grande. Once the Audi stopped, the driver stepped around and stood in front of Young Ham with his arms folded across his barrelled chest.

"Please, Young Ham," Juan said as he stepped out, "every day I wake, I think this is the day for me to die."

He signaled for his security to frisk Young Ham. Once cleared, they entered the house together. The interior was immaculate and heavily guarded by two fearless German Shepherds. There was no other family visible. Just business.

Young Ham got straight to it. He laid out Pop's plan to counteract Ormiga before the new leadership cemented itself.

"You have a chance to make it right with Franco, with yourself, and most of all… Felipe."

At the mention of PePe's name, Juan stiffened. When he heard that Ormiga had taken over as Magnate-Rey, his face darkened instantly.

"That little spineless turd replaces his grandfather?" Juan snapped. "They call him Ormiga because all de women back home laugh and say he has an ant's penis. This is very dangerous what ye plan to do. We could both be killed if they do not believe ye. I will need time to think."

Young Ham understood the hesitation. But he disagreed. Juan knew the game better than most. Even in a dirty world where rules were meant to be broken, there were still lines that had to be respected. Without Juan, there was no second plan.

So Young Ham waited.

He slept the entire flight back. Another passenger tapped his arm when they landed. Once off the plane, he rented a vehicle, gassed it up, and hit the highway.

There was someone he hadn't visited in far too long. And before he moved another piece on the board, he needed to see them.

For My Niggas On Lock

Three Rivers Federal Institution in Victoria, Texas, was where Stacks was serving his fifteen-year bid. He had bulked up fast from eating good and lifting free iron, his body solid and prison-sculpted. His dreads had grown long, hanging down his back, and when he stepped into the visitation room, he carried himself like confinement hadn't broken him.

He flashed diamonds and gold through that grilled smile like he still owned the outside.

"Fam, you still my nigga if you don't get no bigger," Stacks laughed, flexing on Young Ham as they embraced chest to chest.

"And you forever a baller if you don't get no taller," Young Ham shot back, clowning his boy's five-seven frame.

They took a seat at one of the outer tables.

"Yo, seriously," Young Ham said, his tone shifting. "How you holding up?"

The question wasn't really about the bid. It was about Stacks' younger brother. The death. The kind of loss that hits different when you're locked behind concrete and steel and can't even attend the funeral.

"Man... my nigga," Stacks exhaled, still looking dazed by the news. "It's crazy. I still can't believe he gone. Then I think back to the day we was all in Liana's apartment, joking about how the streets end-either you go to jail or die in the game. Ain't no third option. No regrets about this run though. I just wish he ain't take that dirt nap before me."

The two of them went quiet for a moment, remembering old stories and backyard hustles before the guards walked by and told them to keep it down. Neither of them was tripping over the guard's warning, and kept right on enjoying themselves.

As the minutes ticked down, Stacks' smile faded. The playful energy drained out of him.

"Let me know something, hood," he said, his voice lower now. "Tell me it look like we even."

Stacks tried to mask the pain, but his jaw tightened when he spoke. His little brother was in the sky, and the one responsible was still breathing.

"You ain't gotta ask, Brick," Young Ham said firmly. "Rest assured, I'm on it. Either you gon' hear about it… or you gon' read about it. Whichever hit first."

He didn't raise his voice. He didn't have to.

Stacks studied Young Ham's face, searching for hesitation. He didn't find any. The guards signaled the end of visitation. Their chairs scraped against the floor. The two of them stood and embraced again, this time longer.

"Stay solid," Stacks muttered.

"Always," Young Ham replied.

Young Ham walked out of Three Rivers with an obligation heavier than before. Debts aren't always collected financially. Some debts are written in blood.

Say Hello To My World

Young Ham pushed the weight of the world to the side and dedicated the day to his woman. He and Monique dined at an upscale restaurant near downtown, overlooking Lady Bird Lake. The view stretched across the water and into the city's skyline, creating the kind of atmosphere couples dream about when they imagine romance done right.

"Mmm, this is delicious," Monique said, slicing into her veal chops before spearing another piece and feeding it to him. "You like?"

"I do," Young Ham answered between chews, watching her expression more than the plate.

"I do too," she replied smoothly, looking into his eyes with intention.

He smiled back at her. "You already are."

Earlier that morning, before arriving at the restaurant, the two had toured a six-acre, 4.5-million-dollar estate discreetly positioned at the top of Bee Cave Mountain. The property overlooked the city like it belonged to someone who planned on owning more than just real estate.

"What you decide on the house?" Young Ham asked, circling back to it.

"Oh, yeah," she sighed. "I fell in love the second I saw the master bedroom balcony view of the city below. But what about you?"

"It don't matter if I sleep under covers or under stars," he replied calmly. "As long as my pockets fat, I'm good. But if it makes you happy… I'm all in."

"And that's why I do," she laughed.

What truly caught Young Ham's attention wasn't just the layout or the land. It was the vault-style garage designed to store an exotic collection. The property even included space marked for a helipad. He didn't own a chopper yet, but the idea of having the option felt like growth only a boss understood.

He set his drink down and signaled the waitress. She returned moments later carrying a silver platter topped with the restaurant's most expensive champagne, two flutes, and a slender black box.

"Here's your order, sir," she smiled, setting everything down before opening the box.

Inside was a sparkling diamond necklace that instantly lit the room. "And this is for you, ma'am."

Monique's eyes said everything before her lips could. As the waitress fastened the necklace around her neck, Young Ham leaned forward.

"Queen, you been by my side since I was laid up on that hospital bed not knowing if I was gon' make it. Now that you've made the decision to accept me as I am, it's time I take you deeper into my world so you understand the life of a hustler firsthand - not that watered-down version they tried to feed you downtown."

Tears gathered in the corners of her eyes.

"King," she said softly, "I never told you this, but when you were in that coma, I went to see your mama before she passed. I wanted to meet the woman who gave birth to the man I was falling in love with."

She reached across the table and took his hand.

"And even though she didn't know who I was at the time, and was too weak to keep her eyes open long, I remember her smiling when she saw me walk in. I held her hand and told her not to worry about you. I promised her I would love and cherish the ground her son walked on, and that I would never let anything separate us."

The commitment was sealed between them.

They finished their meal with a tasting of the restaurant's newest cheesecake, Million Buck Pie, and laughed the night away. But in the back of Young Ham's mind, he knew if Monique truly wanted to wear the crown, she would have to meet the crew first. That was the real test.

They left Stark's full and slightly tipsy before heading back across town to the old condominium. Young Ham had to park on the street because the driveway was lined with vehicles stacked back to back.

"What they got going on in there… a party?" Monique asked.

"Actually," he smirked, "they waiting to see the FBI lady who been taking pictures of them."

She laughed.

"The Cash Keepers are in there?" she asked.

"Yep. Now let me introduce you to the squad them white folks downtown hating on 'cause we got more money than their slave-owning ancestors ever had."

When they stepped through the door, applause erupted. Chase and L shouted, "One-time!" and the room burst into laughter, even Monique.

"What's up, lil' sis?" Big Zeke called out, pulling everyone into a meet-and-greet session.

"Hey, y'all," Monique smiled. "It's good to meet you all. Now can I get everybody together for a group photo?"

The room went dead silent.

"Gotcha!" she laughed.

Moments later, the laughter returned louder than before. Young Ham waited until the energy settled before speaking.

"These three women are special to me and this organization. They play major roles in this family and I wouldn't be where I'm at without their assistance. Thank you, ladies."

He nodded at them before adding, "Kenya and Queen, can y'all give us a minute."

When they stepped aside, Young Ham stood between Monique and Adiva, taking one of each of their hands.

"Do you love me like you say you do?" he asked Monique first.

"Baby, you know I do," she answered sincerely. "I just threw in the towel on my career to prove it's you and me against the world."

He turned to Adiva.

"Do you love me like you say you do?"

"Young Ham," she replied calmly, "words can't express the connection we share. But if I must answer plainly, I love you like I do - not just like I say I do."

He nodded.

"And I love you both. That's why I brought y'all face to face. It's time y'all learn to coexist. Adiva, you already knew about Monique. This ain't new."

He looked directly at Monique.

"I told you I was gon' expose my entirety. You're my woman. But Adiva… she's been with me from a different angle. I'm not putting one above the other. I'm just telling the truth."

Monique studied his face. He wasn't joking.

"I'm speechless," she admitted. "But I've heard you say many times the body never lies. So I'm listening to my heart and placing it in your hands. Just don't mishandle it."

Later that evening…

While waiting for the house closing to finalize, Young Ham and Monique were staying at the Radisson Hotel. That's when his phone rang. Big Zeke was calling from The Car Wash on MLK.

"It's been real, boss," Big Zeke said. "But I'm 'bout to do Boo-Nanny something real bad in front of everybody for blazing my people."

"Look, Zeke," Young Ham answered evenly. "We already took too many losses. Think, my nigga! We gon' touch that fool when the time right."

"I hear you, dog. But my trigger finger itch every time I think about how he dropped my kinfolk and still out here dragging his nuts."

"Trust me," Young Ham replied. "I want him laid out too. But we gotta move like phantoms. When they don't know how it's coming, that's what put fear in a man's heart."

"So what's the play?"

"It's called the stall tactic. In their minds, we tucked our tails. They thinking we just some money getters who ain't 'bout that life because we ain't responded yet."

"So we letting this ride a whole year like with yo kinfolk Base?"

"Not at all," Young Ham corrected. "The Cavanaugh brothers gon' be dealt with. And when we move, we fracturing their whole hood."

He paused.

"And since Boo-Nanny pulled the trigger, we gon' snatch him up and let you decide how it end."

Big Zeke went quiet before responding. "Alright. We've come this far. I'm rolling with you."

After the call ended, Young Ham leaned back in the hotel chair. Truth be told, he didn't have a piece of a plan yet. He just needed Big Zeke calm. The crew couldn't afford another loss, but he knew he wouldn't be able to leash Big Zeke forever.

Minutes later, his phone rang again.

"Young Ham," the voice said. "I have decided to join forces with you in taking down Ormiga. We can leave for Colombia tomorrow, if you like."

Young Ham didn't smile but he did stand up. The next move was bigger than the block.

Boss Moves

Bosses, underbosses, hitmen, and cartel soldiers filled the interior of the Colombia estate. Before entering, Juan had leaned in close to the right ears, reminding the men on the ground of the respect owed to the late Domino and the bloodline that still carried weight.

Colombia had three major drug-trafficking cartels, The Triad, and every major figure was present. Manuel "Manny" Cortez of VC, representing Villavicencio. Luis Armando, boss of BC, representing Bogotá. And lastly, Ormiga from Medellín, head of the Manate-Rey family.

Smiles were thin and handshakes were scarce. The decade-long war between the families had left scars too deep for pleasantries. Money could make peace temporary, but it had not erased mistrust.

And today wasn't about profit.

Today was about "over-throne."

In gangster terminology, it was impeachment. In their world, it meant something far more permanent. If found guilty, you didn't step down. You didn't retire. You were removed. Forever.

When all parties were seated, the meeting began around a massive circular table. Present were the three reigning bosses, Juan, Young Ham, and Willy, Franco's father, representing his deceased son's stake.

Traditionally, this room was reserved for Colombian shareholders only. But Young Ham possessed Franco's lighter, the Magnate-Rey certificate, granting him partial leeway. That alone wasn't enough. That's why Juan and Willy had entered with him. They carried the skin. Young Ham carried the voice.

Ormiga sat across from Young Ham, staring him down with murderous contempt. The feeling was mutual. One rule governed this assembly: no firearms. Every man had been thoroughly searched before entering the mansion.

"Can someone explain to me why we are here today," Manny spoke up calmly, "and why I am missing little Tom-Tom's baseball game for this?"

"Why we are here is ridiculous," Ormiga replied coldly, his grey eyes cutting across the table. "The thought of my leadership being questioned by an American is disgraceful to this country."

"Ormiga," Luis said evenly, "we follow Triad procedure. With respect, allow us to hear the matter."

Luis gestured toward Young Ham.

Young Ham rose slowly, clearing his throat.

"First off," he began, steady and controlled, "thank you, gentlemen, for allowing me to stand among men of your caliber. I don't come here to disrespect nobody. I come here to present information so y'all can decide for yourselves what's real and what's fake."

"How dare we let this mayate embarrass us with American ghetto talk," Ormiga shouted.

Luis shot him a look sharp enough to cut glass.

"It is you who are staining our customs with uncontrolled behavior," Luis said firmly. "This is unacceptable."

Ormiga leaned back slightly, but his eyes never left Young Ham.

"When I first connected with my niggas, or mayates." Young Ham continued, "I vowed to lead them with loyalty, honor, and respect. No snake behavior. No backdoor dealings. In my country, that's called player-hating. And that's exactly what Ormiga been doing since day one."

"Lies!" Ormiga jumped to his feet. "What proof do you have to back this nonsense? If I had my gun, I would put a bullet through your mouth for speaking on my name."

Manny slammed his fist onto the table.

"Enough. If there is evidence, let it be presented."

Young Ham nodded to Juan.

Juan stepped forward with a black folder, opened it, and spread its contents across the table. Photographs. Every boss leaned forward.

One image showed Ormiga's men at the open trunk of a vehicle he had deliberately overpacked. Another showed millions in cash being exchanged into the hands of Ormiga's associates - money meant for Cash Keepers distribution. A final image captured their restaurant encounter.

Luis adjusted in his seat.

"You gullible coward," Ormiga growled at Juan. "Where did you get these?"

The room shifted. Power had begun to tilt.

"Capo, this one is stamped with the date you told me you were in Bolivia."

Ormiga made one last stab at saving face. "Can't you see these are fakes. You are not believing an American over me…are you?"

Young Ham unclasped his recorder watch, set it in the middle of the table and pressed play. Their conversation at Mama Diva's was shortened when Ormiga slammed a fist on top of the device, smashing it to pieces.

But it was of no use. Manny and Luis had heard enough. Ormiga was guilty as charged. With a snap of their fingers, four guerilla built men in suits sprung into action. In a worthless effort, Ormiga struggled with the heavy men but was easily overtaken.

Ormiga's collapse sent a ripple through the room that no one dared acknowledge out loud. Once restrained, gagged, and removed through the side exit like yesterday's trash, the power structure shifted instantly.

Outside, Ormiga's body was flung inside the trunk of a foreign vehicle. The jungle would decide what happened to him next, but inside that estate, the throne was already vacant.

Later, at Franco's family home, Young Ham understood the weight of what he had just inherited. He entered behind Willy and Juan and was greeted at the door by a soft-spoken Colombian woman who didn't speak a word of English. Still, her eyes studied him carefully. If she welcomed him into her home, then she had already measured his character in ways language couldn't translate.

Franco's two sisters stepped forward after their mother, offering respectful handshakes. Young Ham kept his composure, but he couldn't deny what he saw. They were both graceful in looks, and dressed in a Colombian way that didn't beg for attention but commanded it anyway.

After dinner, once Young Ham had eaten more than he intended. Willy dismissed the women from the table. The men needed to speak freely.

"Young Ham," Willy began slowly, his accent heavy but steady, "you are a good man... and very brave. And wise." He paused, weighing the next words. "The life my son lived... it is no good for family. I am sorry, but I cannot put my family in danger."

Young Ham nodded.

"Thank you, Willy. You showed up big today," he replied sincerely.

With Ormiga removed and the Magnate-Rey chair empty, Luis and Manny agreed that Young Ham had earned the right to fill the seat. But there was a condition. Beyond respect, beyond reputation, beyond power - there were rules.

The Triad constitution was strict. A shareholder could be of no race other than Colombian. The law had been written long before Young Ham ever stepped foot in their country. To maneuver around it without violating tradition, the remaining bosses agreed to a compromise: Young Ham could orchestrate American-based dealings but only through a Colombian asset.

No Colombian front, no throne.

The realization hit him heavier than Ormiga's accusations ever did. Without a solid connection, he and his team would be right back at square one, scrambling for a reliable supplier, and rebuilding from scratch. Juan was out of the question. After killing his best friend, he wanted no part of the game anymore.

For a moment, it felt like the victory had an expiration date.

Just as Young Ham began mentally preparing to return to the States and explain to his crew that the window had closed, Franco's youngest sister stepped into the kitchen from behind the dividing wall where she had been quietly listening.

"Papa… I will go," Juliet said.

Her English was flawless. Too flawless. Young Ham would've bet money she didn't know how to speak it.

"Juliet! No!" Willy barked immediately, panic flashing across his face. He already knew what America did to Colombian children who tasted opportunity.

"Francisco would want me to, Papa," she insisted, her voice trembling but determined.

"Think about Mama, Juli. How you will hurt her," he pleaded.

"But Papa," she pressed, "I want to finish my brother's legacy - what he was robbed of. This is our lineage. I must."

Young Ham had heard enough. The back-and-forth was no longer about emotion. It was about destiny.

Juliet's eyes locked onto him as he stood and approached her. He recognized the spark instantly. It was a dangerous mixture of admiration and ambition. He reached into his pocket and placed twenty big faces into her palm, closing her fingers around it.

"Have a safe trip," he told her quietly.

Then he turned to Willy.

"You have my word," Young Ham said firmly. "I'll take care of your daughter with my own life."

$ $ $ $ $

The condo was quiet when Young Ham returned. The long trip back had drained him. Driving to the hotel seemed miles away, and he needed rest. Victory still replayed in his mind. Colombia had been about control. But being back home, it was about survival.

He planned to call Monique in the morning and let her know he'd made it back safely. While he'd been gone, she'd been watching his puppies, Cash and Flow, even though she wasn't much of a dog person.

The house was silent. Great. He didn't need anything else tonight. Just a pillow and peace. Toya must've gone over to Adiva's after work, something she did often.

Chase, L, and Black Jesus were never hard to find. They had been moving product hand-over-fist lately. Young Ham rarely interfered unless it was the weekend and they were counting money together on the living room floor.

Climbing the stairs to his old room, he set his pistol, keys, and a bankroll on the nightstand before collapsing onto the bed. He was out within minutes, breathing heavy and snoring lightly.

He didn't know how long he had been asleep. But when he opened his eyes, something felt wrong. A big-barrel gun was staring him dead in the face. Young Ham's eyes flicked toward the nightstand.

"Try it, nigga," Black Jesus said calmly. "And get your wig pushed backwards."

Black Jesus grabbed the burner off the nightstand and tossed it across the room.

"Get up," he ordered. "So I can at least let you die on your feet."

Young Ham slid off the bed slowly, keeping the mattress between them.

"What the fuck is wrong with you?" he asked evenly. "You done started back smoking that shit again?"

Black Jesus threw his hands up, pacing.

"What's wrong with me? You is what's wrong with me. Every time I try to school my son, he run to you. How I'm supposed to be his father when all he do is look up to you? I'm sick of this. And we ending it tonight."

Young Ham stayed calm.

"Black Jesus, you talking crazy," he said. "You gotta give it a chance. He ain't a kid no more, dog. Stop trippin' and let's go talk to him."

"Tripping?" Black Jesus laughed bitterly. "You groomed him. You turned him into you. You ain't no leader. You a manipulator."

Young Ham took a slow step forward.

"You think this a game? You really think I'm playing with you? I'm about to erase you out of Chase's life forever."

Boom. Boom. Boom.

Gunfire ripped through the room and silence followed. Young Ham stood frozen for a split second before registering what had just happened.

The shots hadn't come from Black Jesus. They had come from the doorway. And when Young Ham looked up. He wasn't alone.

The Ultimate Gameplan

The first gunshot rang so loud it felt like it cracked the air in half. Young Ham had dropped to the floor clutching his chest, convinced that the bullets had found him. His ears rang violently. The room spun. When his vision cleared, he looked toward the doorway.

Toya stood there with a smoking gun in her hand.

Black Jesus lay face down on the carpet, blood spreading across the once snow-white fibers, soaking through like spilled paint.

Toya hadn't planned it. She'd left work early that day with a stomach ache and fallen asleep downstairs. The arguing upstairs woke her. At first she assumed it was Chase and L back on the game, loud and reckless. But then she heard Black Jesus' voice talking crazy, and something about his words rattled her.

She crept up the stairs quietly, heart pounding in her chest. When she reached the doorway and saw Black Jesus holding Young Ham at gunpoint, her body moved before her fear could catch up. She grabbed the pistol off the floor, and fired.

"You just killed yo brother's daddy," Young Ham said, pushing himself up slowly.

Unmoved, Toya stepped forward and fired again into Black Jesus' back.

"My brother always told me we ain't have no daddy," she said coldly. "So fuck him."

The room went silent except for the ringing in Young Ham's ears. Neighbors had already called 911, and the police came fast.

The condo wasn't tucked inside the hood. It sat close enough to know the streets, but far enough outside hood lines to get special attention when something went wrong.

APD and EMS responded in a flash, flooding the place with flashing lights. Officers snapped gloves on, and began asking questions and clicking cameras.

When they told Young Ham they were taking Toya in until they could "sort it out," something triggered inside him.

"That's straight bullshit," he snapped. "He pulled a gun on me in my sleep. He was threatening to kill me."

They weren't trying to hear it. A rookie officer grabbed Toya by the arm to lead her to the cruiser.

"Get the fuck off me," she barked, jerking away. "I can walk."

The rookie tensed, hand hovering near his pepper spray.

"Calm down, Warren," an older Black officer stepped in. "Ma'am, let's not make this harder than it needs to be."

"Whatever!" Toya exhaled and walked to the back seat herself.

Young Ham met her at the door before she got in.

"Don't worry about nothing," he said low. "You'll have a lawyer in the morning. I'm coming down there first thing."

She looked at him hard.

"The last time I got in the back of one of these," she said quietly, "they locked me up in a foster home. This time they gon' find somewhere worse."

The door shut.

And just like that, she was gone.

$ $ $ $ $

Toya wasn't exaggerating. Juvenile court made an example out of her, sentencing her to the Texas Youth Commission for two years. She was transferred to an all-girls facility in Corsicana.

Young Ham was the only adult family member allowed on her visitation list. Once a month, he loaded up the boys and made the drive. No excuses. No missed trips.

Then one Saturday, on the way back from a visit, his phone lit up with an unfamiliar 817 area code.

"Who this?"

"It's me, Young Ham. Juliet."

He swerved to the shoulder immediately and stepped out the car, pacing so he wouldn't lose signal.

"I'm here. Where you at?"

"I'm in Mexico right now, but we're heading to Dallas next. Can you pick me up there?"

"Of course. You still got some of the money I gave you?"

"Yeah, but it'll be gone once I pay the driver."

"Don't stress that. Call me when you touch Dallas. I'll already be there."

There was a pause on the line.

"And Young Ham… I belong to you now."

$ $ $ $ $

Four hours later, he was in North Texas. Chase and L had never been that far upstate before, so the trip felt like something bigger than business. They made a few stops in South Dallas, hitting the Galleria, grabbing some food, and letting the boys burn off energy. But mostly they waited for the call.

Outside a sneaker store, Young Ham ran into Dino, a face from way back. Back when they were just kids in TYC trying to look and act tougher than they were.

"Damn, Young Ham!" Dino called out. "I knew that was you!"

They shook hands. Dino was a stack taller and had filled out since state school, but still had that same loud energy.

"Dino?" Young Ham asked. "What the business, playboy?"

Dino grinned. "Getting them dollars like I told you I was gon' do. Tell me something good though."

Young Ham studied him carefully. He remembered Dino's mouth used to be bigger than his hustle.

"I said if we ever crossed paths, we was gon' make it happen. So whatever you paying for the raw, I'ma go a thousand cheaper."

111

They set a meeting for the following week. Dino peeled off in a bright green Lambo, engine screaming louder than a F-1 race car.

Later, while eating at William's Chicken, Young Ham got another call with instructions on where to pick Juliet up.

When he pulled up, she looked nothing like the princess girl from Colombia. Her hair was greasy and matted. Her clothes clung to her wrong, and the smell hit them before she even stepped close.

Chase made a face.

"Who this bitch?" he muttered.

L laughed under his breath. "Why you picking up this smoker?"

Young Ham shot them both a look that said cut it out.

"Y'all chill," he said quietly. "This the reason y'all gon' drive Bentleys before twenty-one."

Juliet approached with her head lowered.

"I'd hug you," she said softly, "but I'm ashamed to look like this in a king's presence."

Young Ham lifted her chin gently.

"Pick yo head up," he told her. "I know a diamond when I see one."

Then he opened the car door.

"Welcome to my country."

Element of Surprise

Juliet had been a rough fit from the start. Young Ham thought tucking her away quietly until she found her footing would be simple, but he underestimated her. She listened, but underneath that obedience she had her own agenda in mind. Juliet didn't follow instructions from other women.

He had dropped her under the Nigerian Trio's roof and told Adiva to keep an eye on her. Take her shopping. Get her hair and nails done. Introduce her to the city properly. Make her comfortable but not powerful. Yet adding another female to a house already full of personalities was gasoline near a lit matchstick .

Too many cats and no dogs.

"This heifer gon' make me wring her neck," Adiva snapped one evening, folding her arms tight across her chest. "She walkin' around like she Queen Elizabeth. Had the nerve to catch an attitude when I told her to help clean up."

Young Ham leaned back, studying the situation.

"Don't trip yet, babygirl," he said evenly. "We still building. Tomorrow, go put six months rent down on that spot I showed you. I'll deal with her when I get back from visiting Pop."

Adiva exhaled slow. "I'm cool. I just know if she wasn't here for a purpose, I would've dragged her skinny self right back to the airport."

Young Ham didn't respond. Because truthfully, he didn't fully trust Juliet either.

$ $ $ $ $

Pop sat across from him at visitation, fingers folded like a game master contemplating a risky move.

"So how it go?" Pop asked.

"It worked out," Young Ham said, letting a small smile tug at his mouth. "Came back with more than I left with. Franco's sister volunteered herself. Said she wants to carry out her brother's legacy."

Pop's eyes narrowed slightly.

"Correct me if I'm wrong," he said slowly, "but in order for you to secure that chain of business, you needed somebody Colombian to front it."

"Exactly."

"And this girl just… stepped up?"

Young Ham hesitated. He didn't like that Pop always heard more than what was said.

"Yeah. She jumped at the opportunity."

Pop leaned forward. "Don't stick yo dick in this broad."

Young Ham frowned. "What?"

"She ain't decide that day she was goin' to America. That was brewing already. That girl got her own plans. Women move different when money and power mix."

Young Ham looked down at the metal table. Pop wasn't wrong. Juliet had moved with urgency, and was too willing. But the game recognized the game. And that's what intrigued him most about her.

"Either way," Young Ham replied, "the business lined up."

Pop studied him one more time before nodding slowly. "Just don't confuse loyalty with opportunity. But what's with your homeboy's death?"

"Ain't nothing," he said, brushing it off. Pop never seemed to miss nothing going on in the streets.

"Nah, son. It's far from that." he scolded. "Every piece on the chessboard is sacrificial…except the king. Use the influence of power and quit letting off brand niggas get under you."

114

Trusting Black Jesus almost cost Young Ham dearly. Never again. He looked up in time to see a guard knock twice on the table. "Times up, Hamilton."

$$\$ \$ \$ \$ \$$$

The ride back from visiting Pop gave him too much time to think. When he pulled up at the Nigerian Trio's spot, there was an unfamiliar vehicle in the driveway. Jalil had flown in.

Inside, Jalil greeted him like a brother but respected him like a business man.

"Look, yo," Jalil said, loosening his tie. "I got a problem when people play with my money."

Young Ham leaned against the counter. "Talk to me."

"No knock on what you do," Jalil continued, "but selling dope ain't my favorite industry. Still, a hundred grand to make a phone call is hard to ignore, but we'll get back to that later. What I'm hearing is there's static in your backyard."

Young Ham's jaw tightened slightly. "Ja, that's good looking. But whatever situation you referring to gon' get handled. Trust me."

"Don't feel betrayed but me and my sister talk about everything. I'm here because in order for us to move forward, we must put the distractions behind us."

"So what you getting at?" Young Ham asked.

"If you give the word," Jalil said calmly, "I'll fly in a gang of Zowie dread heads from Brooklyn and do a clean sweep. Make it loud enough that nobody ever tests you again."

Young Ham thought about that. Outside muscle meant no sweat and no emotional ties. But it also meant inviting wolves into your own yard.

"And what's that cost me?"

"Two-fifty. Problem solved."

Young Ham had built his name brick by brick. Letting another man solve his problems chipped at his ego, but he consented anyway.

"Do it."

Jalil grinned slightly. "Let's focus on profits…not problems."

As they walked toward the door, Young Ham paused. "What does Zowie mean?"

Jalil's smile widened. "Element of surprise."

Bad News Travels Fast

"Ninety-eight… ninety-nine… one hundred."

"Mail call, Mr. Hudson."

Stacks grabbed the stack of Austin American-Statesman papers Ms. Murray handed him after finishing his last set of knuckle push-ups. Sweat glistened across his shoulders, his muscles still tight from the burn.

"Appreciate you, Ms. Murray," he said, flashing that diamond grin.

She lingered a second longer than necessary, eyes dragging across his frame. "You stay outta trouble," she muttered.

Stacks smirked. Trouble wasn't something you stayed out of. It was something you survived. Back on his bunk, he flipped to the Metro & State-his favorite section, outside of Comics-and froze.

The headline stretched bold across the page: A DISASTROUS ACT AGAINST A NEIGHBORHOOD.

Below it, images of burned houses, shattered glass, and bodies covered beneath white sheets littered the streets of the terror struck neighborhood. Stacks leaned back against the wall and read aloud under his breath.

Residents reported being awakened at six a.m. by rapid gunfire and explosions that shook entire blocks. Authorities described it as an "act of war," allegedly tied to a gang affiliated with a street known as The Hill. Police are still investigating searches for masked individuals armed with military-style weapons. Furthermore, the girlfriend of Percy Cavanaugh has reported that her children's father and her were asleep in bed when a group of masked men ramshackled their home, beating her and Mr. Cavanaugh unconscious. A missing persons report has been filed after she informed officers that Mr. Cavanaugh has not been seen since.

Stacks folded the paper slowly. "Rest easy, lil' bro," he whispered toward the ceiling. "It's forever Cash Keepers."

$ $ $ $ $

Two weeks later, Young Ham was running things from Big Zeke's newly rented townhouse. The air inside was thick with smoke and fresh money energy.

"You straight now, big homie?" Young Ham asked.

"Fo' sho'," Big Zeke replied, grinning darkly. "I handled that nigga like a runaway slave."

Young Ham didn't need the details. The tone told him enough.

"Good. Now it's time to level up," Young Ham said. "I need you to come out the Bricks and place L in yo spot. Let our soldiers handle the front line market. I need you over distribution."

Big Zeke inhaled deeply from his roll-up. He loved meeting the streets head on. "I ain't built to sit behind a desk."

"You ain't," Young Ham agreed. "You built to make sure our corners stay fed. Apartments stay stocked. Blocks stay moving. That's bigger action if you think about it."

Big Zeke nodded.

"And what about them three you was 'posed to promote off the block?" Young Ham pressed.

"They good. Lil Lucky holding Elmeridge down. K-Dawg got the Marshalls jumping, and the shorty Paige locking Kingston Village down tight. Weekly profits looking good."

"Nice," Young Ham agreed. "Our five project grounds gon' need constant maintenance."

"Huh?"

"Yeah. Muncy recognized the potential of connecting with us. That's one more area for you to cover."

"Bet!"

Young Ham wasn't just expanding territory. He was stretching the system.

$ $ $ $ $

The money was flowing heavier than ever, and Juliet had adapted with alarming speed. She placed herself in a high-dollar gated community residence without consulting Young Ham. She burned through a twenty-thousand-dollar monthly budget recklessly.

In weeks, she reformed into an Americanized prima donna. She had a designer addiction, and somehow polished her attitude to match.

Juliet was nineteen with no driving skills. Young Ham tolerated showing her the ropes because he was burnt out chauffeuring her around, and that was often.

"Come inside," she said one evening after a driving lesson. "I got something for you."

"Juliet, don't get in this house and start playin'."

She had thrown herself at him every chance she got since coming to America.

"I'm not, daddy." she pouted. "I got a surprise for real."

He followed her inside. She put on her best strut, making sure he noticed her thighs were thicker than before.

"Wait here. I'll be back."

The house was immaculate. Black furniture decorated the living room's space. Expensive art covered the walls all around, whispering power in a foreign language.

"Open it and tell me if you like them." She handed him a jewelry box, and flopped down on the couch beside him, grinning like a preschooler.

Inside were two-carat diamond studs. He had lost his last pair and hadn't thought of buying new ones.

"These legit."

"You a king," she said. "Kings should look like it. Here's the other half of your gift."

119

Juliet raised from the couch and undressed. Her matching lingerie challenged Pop's warning. Don't stick yo dick in that broad.

"See, you hard headed." he scolded. "Told you in the car don't get in here and start them games."

She stepped closer.

"Please, Young Ham." she begged, pressing together her firm breast. "I want you to be my first."

"I'm not fucking you, Juliet. So stop asking."

She wasn't taking no for an answer. She squatted between his legs and rested her elbows on his thighs. Her small hand traveled inside his basketball shorts, and massaged his tool. He didn't protest when she sprung it free and kissed the tip lightly.

Pop's warning echoed faintly in his mind, but Juliet's warm mouth spoke louder than his conscience.

"Since I'm on dick-down restriction. Teach me how to eat your pickle."

Ups and Downs

Pop warned him not to stick his dick in Juliet, but he never clarified the "in" part.

In the heat of the moment, Young Ham let temptation overrule discipline. Juliet slurped him slow and confident, like she had studied oral pleasure the way other people studied college courses.

She claimed she had a virgin throat, but the way she performed said otherwise. Still, he slipped and let it happen. And in doing so, he crossed a line that entangled business and pleasure - something he knew better than to mix. Once that boundary cracked, everything else cracked with it.

Now that Juliet had planted herself stateside, quarterly shipments rolled in through freight like clockwork. Jalil ordered a hundred a month for his upstate boys, each head bringing in twenty thousand. He wired two million like magic every cycle, bouncing the dirty cash through layers of safeguard accounts untraceable to authorities. On the surface, operations were running smoothly and profitable.

The only thing unstable was the household. If Adiva and Juliet could learn to coexist, life would feel less stressful. Instead, Young Ham found himself once again in Adiva's bedroom, listening to the latest fallout between the two women.

"Foreal," Adiva snapped, calling him by his real name the way she did when she was heated. "I'm tired of holding back from putting my foot in that girl's ass."

"Why y'all can't ever seem to get along?" he asked, already knowing the answer would be one-sided.

"It ain't me. I know you gave her some dick and now she walking around like she top tier. Thinking she can sit where I sit. But what she don't realize is I'm irreplaceable. She ain't."

Young Ham fought the smile tugging at his mouth. Adiva wasn't speaking out of jealousy - she was behaving territorially. There was a difference.

"What happened this time?"

"She came for her allowance and acted like I was taking too long counting it. I told her if she didn't want to wait, she could come back after my hair appointment. She ain't like that so she got in her car without her money. Then rolled her window down talking shit, saying I was a no-good number two bitch."

"Look," he said finally, "from here on out, I'll deal with Juliet so you don't have to worry 'bout y'all being in the same room."

"Please do," Adiva replied. "'Cause she got one more time, and I'm gon' bless her with a land of the free ass whoopings."

$ $ $ $ $

After leaving Adiva, he headed east, cutting through familiar streets before calling it a night. Givens Park looked the same as always. He honked at a few regular faces crowded around a dice game, like nothing else in the world mattered.

He kept driving.

When he pulled up at the new spot, Cash and Flow met him at the door, barking and jumping like they hadn't seen him in months. For four-month-old pups, they were already oversized, thick in the shoulders and heavy in the paws.

"What's up, black butterfly?" Young Ham asked, sliding behind Monique and wrapping his arms around her waist.

"Boy, move before this hot grease pop on you," she said without turning. "And when we having our housewarming?"

"Whenever my baby ready. You really want all yo' crazy family over here?"

She turned on her heels. "Don't do me. Your people the only ones crazy. Now go answer your phone before I really go there."

Cash and Flow trotted behind him as he moved back into the guest room just in time to catch the call before voicemail.

"Yeah, what's up?"

"Young Ham!" Queen's voice cracked. "Adiva got into a car wreck after she left the house earlier. We at Seton Hospital. They just took her to ICU."

Everything in him froze.

Fifteen minutes later, Young Ham and Monique rushed through the hospital doors, finding Kenya and Queen sitting outside intensive care, faces streaked with tears.

Kenya shot up the second she saw him. "These doctors acting like they can't talk. We been here an hour and ain't nobody telling us nothing!"

Queen stayed seated, holding herself together but barely. "They won't say what's going on."

Monique stepped forward, hugging both of them tight. Her eyes were glossy, but she stayed strong.

Young Ham swallowed whatever panic was rising in his chest. "She gon' be alright," he said - not because he was certain, but because they needed to hear comfort.

A doctor stepped into the hallway and approached them slowly, face solemn. "Hi, I'm Dr. Evans."

Young Ham stepped forward first.

"I want you all to understand," the doctor began carefully, "she's in there fighting for her life. The collision caused severe trauma to her brain."

"Skip that shit," Kenya snapped. "Is she gon' make it or not?"

"Doc," Queen said, standing now and holding onto Kenya. "We just need to know her chances."

Dr. Evans shifted uncomfortably. "Right now, I don't have many answers. My team is doing everything we can to stabilize her...and the baby."

Silence fell.

"The baby?" they all said at once.

Young Ham stepped closer, confused. "What baby you talking about, doc?"

Dr. Evans looked at his chart. "It's been confirmed through multiple tests that Ms. Oladipo is three and a half months pregnant."

EPILOGUE

One year later…

Young Ham pulled the hoodie over his head, letting the light rain tap softly against the fabric. He stood over Adiva's gravestone, composed on the outside-but the weight in his chest hadn't eased a bit since the day she left. He exhaled slowly and spoke.

It ain't been the same since you left, baby girl… not even close. The Nigerian Trio is no more without you. Kenya and Queen sold the house, and walked away from everything we built. They ain't chasing money no more. Tell you the truth, they ain't chasing nothing. Yeah… I know. Crazy, right? Told you it wasn't the same.

He shifted his weight as the rain picked up just a little.

Besides that, yo girl Toya still holding it down. She took what happened to you hard. Real hard. But she down there giving them people hell like she supposed to. She'll be home next year around this time.

His voice got firmer.

The Cash Keepers are still making it move how we want it to move. You already know we run the streets. Aye… you remember Chase and L? Them lil' niggas grown now. Calling themselves Young World, and making noise like they got something to prove. They a trip…but getting paid, no doubt. And Juliet. Yeah… I know how you felt about her.

But she still a part of this… whether anybody like it or not.

He looked up toward the sky. It felt like the rain started coming down harder

Don't be tripping up there. You know how this lifestyle goes. Sometimes I sit back and wonder what if that crash ain't take you out. What if you would've made it? What if you were here now carrying my child.

That one thought hit him. He swallowed the grief and continued.

I'm running low on words now, but I had to pull up to talk to you. Get it off my chest so I can keep it pushing.

He reached into his front pouch and pulled out a single red rose. He knelt and placed the flower gently at the base of her headstone. He stood back up.

So I'm gon' let you rest.…Until next month.

Across the cemetery grounds, past the tree line where the road meets the grass. A black SUV sat parked in the shadows, engine running. Inside, two men watched Young Ham's silhouette moving through the rain. The one in the passenger seat lowered a pair of binoculars.

"That's him."

The driver didn't respond right away, he just nodded, never taking his eyes off Young Ham.

"Been watching him build for a long time," he finally said. "Brick by brick."

"He adapted faster than we expected," the passenger said, almost impressed. "Took some hits along the way but didn't fold."

The driver smirked.

"But he's still controlled by a system he don't even know exists."

"Most of 'em don't."

"Every move he ever thought was his own…had already been calculated."

Rain tapped harder against the windshield, blurring the view just enough to make Young Ham look like a ghost.

Young Ham reached his car.

The passenger watched him for a long moment. "The question ain't whether he ready or not," he said. "It's whether he survives."

Then the passenger reached into his coat and pulled out a small phone. He pressed one button and held it to his ear. "We're in position," he said.

A voice on the other end responded coldly. "Let him breathe…for now."

The driver shifted the SUV into gear and rolled forward, vanishing like they had never been there.

To be continued…
Cash Keepers 3
Coming Soon!

ABOUT THE AUTHOR

D'Shon Major is an urban fiction author who writes "dope-tales" drawn from real experiences, and unseen consequences of the street-rooted grind called the GAME. He is currently incarcerated but unapologetically in pursuance of something greater than his circumstances. Cash Keepers is a reflection of lived moments, hard lessons, and the reality behind the hustle.

www.ingramcontent.com/pod-product-compliance
Lightning Source LLC
Chambersburg PA
CBHW051127160726
47997CB00018B/803